FAIRY TALE
REFORM SCHOOL

SWITCHED

Jen Calonita

SCHOLASTIC INC.

ISBN 978-1-338-28890-2

12 11 10 9 8 7 6 5 4 3 2 1   18 19 20 21 22 23

Printed in the U.S.A.   40

First Scholastic printing, March 2018

Series design by Regina Flath
Cover image by Michael Heath/Shannon Associates

For my godson, Gianluca Campagna.
I can't wait till you're old enough for us to read this together.

It's all about the climb.

Happily Ever After Scrolls

Brought to you by FairyWeb—Enchantasia's
Number One News Source!

Fairy Tale Reform School Has a New Library and Two New Teachers

by Coco Collette

Fairy Tale Reform School is buzzing with excitement this week as the school prepares to welcome two new staff members, one of whom will be running the school's shiny, new library! "Headmistress Flora is thankful to her step-daughter, Princess Ella, and the rest of the royal court for generously funding a new library at FTRS," says school spokesmirror Miri.

The mirror is quick to add that the school has always had an extensive book collection but nowhere to put it, and that their new library will include enchanted books. ("I'll let our new librarian explain how they work," Miri says cryptically.) The library, which was built by ELF Construction over the last several months, is in a new wing at the school, which will also include classrooms dedicated to FTRS's new transitional school program—From Mischief-Maker to Model Citizen (also referred to as MMC).

"MMC is for students who have shown significant improvement in their studies and behavior," explains Headmistress Flora. "Rather than be released from FTRS, they have chosen to continue their studies under our tutelage, hoping to learn more about their new 'good' side and how to figure out their future in the kingdom of Enchantasia. We are honored to be able to help them on this journey." The coursework was created after being suggested by star student Gilly Cobbler, who wanted to stay on at FTRS.

Families in Enchantasia know all too well how quickly a child can go from wondrous to wicked. Many parents are still searching for students who decided to leave town with Rumpelstiltskin after he was ousted from his position as FTRS headmaster two months ago. Neither Mr. Stiltskin nor his squad have been heard from since. While there are whispers that many folks were won over by Mr. Stiltskin's fear tactics and hard stance on protecting the kingdom, *HEAS* has learned the royal court did not like the direction in which he was taking FTRS and was pleased to see him gone. "The court was thrilled when several students tricked Stiltskin into giving up his position," says a palace source. To no one's surprise, Gilly Cobbler was among that student group.

To thank them, and Headmistress Flora, the princesses gifted FTRS with a proper library. "We hope all of Enchantasia will delight in seeing FTRS's new library with its many enchanting features," says Princess Ella. "And we couldn't be happier that Headmistress Flora liked our suggestions for new staff." The princess would not reveal the names of the staffers, but says "they are known throughout the lands. We are fortunate they agreed to move to Enchantasia and help us." *HEAS* can't wait to find out who these staffers could be!

Stay tuned for details on FTRS's new teachers!

CHAPTER 1

Read It and Weep

W ho tells a kid to keep out of the library?

As I tap my foot impatiently in the foyer of Fairy Tale Reform School's new library services wing, that's exactly what Headmistress Flora is telling me to do. At least, that's how I interpret the glare she's sending me from across the hall as I huff, sigh, and yawn while she's talking to *Happily Ever After Scrolls*.

Sparkle! Flash!

The reporter covering the library dedication is waving his wand at Headmistress Flora and Princess Ella like he's granting wishes, which I know he's not. What is he doing anyway? And when is Headmistress Flora finally going to cut the blue satin ribbon and open the door?

"Lovely smiles! Just lovely!" the reporter says as he jumps around like the Pied Piper, shaking a large wand that looks like a fallen tree trunk. Flora and her stepdaughter don't seem to mind the fuss. They're standing patiently (*Grrr...*) and smiling brightly in front of the library's oversize stained glass doors.

A library, I should add, that has been dangled in front of us in Miri the Magic Mirror's daily announcements for months. All Miri does anymore is talk about the library. It has rare books that can unlock more than just stories! Books that have a mind of their own! Biographies that contain villains' darkest secrets and potions! Mysterious works gathered from the far reaches of the kingdoms that will teach us things we've never even heard of! And the chance to gain knowledge about Enchantasia's history and all its fairy-tale heroes, villains, and creatures!

Truthfully, I've never been inside a library. Enchantasia Village had a tiny library annex, but the books were ancient and mostly nursery rhymes or trade books about hot cross buns or shoe leathers. Riveting stuff. I can't imagine what the FTRS library will look like. Headmistress Flora and the ELF Construction Company have kept the project top secret. Ollie and I tried to get a sneak peek one night, but Wolfington somehow sensed us coming and sent us back to bed.

The trumpets sound, and a court jester steps forward. "'And now a few words from Princess Ella about the new library,'" he reads from a scroll.

Fairy be. How long is this ceremony going to take? My fairy pet, Wilson, the world's cleverest mouse, sticks his tiny, pink nose out of my blue jumper pocket and squeaks in annoyance. (Technically, fairy pets aren't allowed to leave the classroom, but I've never been a strict rule follower. Neither is Maxine, who houses her duck, Peaches, in our dorm room. The pair have become unlikely friends, like Maxine and me. Who knew an ogre and a human could be so tight?)

"I know," I tell Wilson. "I wish they'd quit with the speeches already. I am dying to get into the library too." Wilson nods his little mouse head as if he understands me.

Ollie clears his throat, and I glare down at him. He's super-short for a pirate.

"Acting impatient is very unbecoming of an RLW," he says, adjusting his bright-pink Royal Ladies-in-Waiting sash, the same one I'm begrudgingly wearing over my jumper.

3

"Dedicating Fairy Tale Reform School's first library is a very big deal." He motions to the hundred or so classmates assembled in the hallway. The entire teaching staff is here too, along with the royal court, reporters, and some fancy folks from the village. "Headmistress Flora wants to make sure it is presented perfectly, since the royal court was gracious enough to give us such an extravagant present."

I roll my eyes. "You know Rapunzel can't hear you being a fancy-schmancy, perfect RLW right now, right?"

"An RLW is always polite." Ollie puffs out his chest, making the writing on his sash easier to read. (Ollie magically crossed out the word *Ladies* and wrote *Lads* next to the pirate skull and crossbones he drew. He's RLW's first male member.) His dark eyes are playful as he shakes his head. "Green does not look good on you, Gilly."

My jaw drops. "You think I'm *jealous*? I am not jealous!"

"Yeah!" Maxine comes to my aid. "Gilly just wants to get in there to find books about Rumpelstiltskin."

Ollie and I slap our hands over Maxine's drooling mouth. I wipe my hand off on my jumper.

"Sorry." Maxine's muddy-gray cheeks turn red. "I forgot no one is supposed to know that."

It's true. We want to find that little monster. Not only did he trick Flora into giving up control of FTRS, but he also conned a group of kids in the village into joining his Stiltskin Squad by promising them they'd run the kingdom, and he convinced some FTRS students to go with him too. Including my younger sister Anna! I know the royal court is looking for him, but no one knows where he is or what he's plotting. All I know is that it can't be good, and I don't want Anna with him when things go bad.

Sparkle! Flash!

The reporter is back at it, wanding the royal court this time. I can't take it anymore.

"What in the name of fairy is that thing anyway?" I grouse.

"It's a Magic 2000," says Jax. As a prince, he's used to long and boring ceremonies. He also doesn't mind ironing his school uniform (mine is wrinkly) and taming his curly, blond hair (my brown hair with the purple skunk stripe is wild today). His normally pale skin has bronzed, thanks to all the Pegasus flying we've been doing, patrolling the FTRS grounds for signs of Rump. So far, we've found none. "The royal court gave one to *HEAS* so they can start taking magical pictures. You should see them." His violet eyes widen. "It's like looking in a mirror! Pete and the Dwarf Police Squad have requested one too. Something about wanting magical pictures to use in Wanted scrolls."

"No scroll is going to find the Rump," says Jocelyn. The Evil Queen's younger sister has arrived fashionably late. She's the only one at our school who gets away with not wearing a uniform. (She wears a blue sash around her moon-and-stars skirt to support the school colors.) She pushes her long, black hair off her pale, almost-white neck. "I told you. When he's ready to destroy the kingdom, he'll pop up."

"That's comforting," says Kayla, her fairy wings fluttering in agitation.

She has more reason than most to get antsy about Stiltskin, who turned her mother and sisters into trees because…well, actually, we don't know why. Kayla's mom says they have very little memory of why he cursed them. Which is yet another roadblock we've faced in finding the little beast.

Kayla's amber eyes lock on the *HEAS* reporter. "That trickster convinced all those kids who went with him that the only way to stop evil is to work by his side!" Her nostrils flare. "They have no clue they're unknowingly helping him try to take over Enchantasia."

"I know!" says a goblin in front of us, listening in to our not-so-quiet conversation. "My roommate, Simeon, was all, like, *This guy listens to me! He wants to keep us safe, give me gold, and make me rich.*" The goblin snorts. "Like Rumpelstiltskin would ever give up any of the gold he makes." The goblin laughs. "Those kids who left with him were so dumb."

"They are not dumb!" I snap, unable to control myself. "Maybe they've realized they made the wrong choice, but now they have no way to get back home. Did you ever think of that?"

Jax puts a hand on my shoulder. The *HEAS* reporter has stopped wanding, and all my professors are looking at me: Professor Wolfington, Professor Harlow, Madame Cleo (visible in a mirror made of sea glass that Professor Blackbeard is holding), and Rapunzel, who runs our Royal Ladies-in-Waiting club. Rapunzel shakes her head at me ever so slightly.

Fiddlesticks.

So much for flying under the radar this morning.

"Sorry!" I shout to the reporter and the others. "Please proceed with the wand thingy. I'll be quiet and not point out that we're running *fifteen minutes* behind schedule and some of us have to be in Wanding: How to Block Curses in an hour."

Headmistress Flora glances at the large clock in the foyer. "Ms. Cobbler makes a valid point. Our new professors will be arriving any moment. We should get the ribbon cutting underway."

There is a murmur of excitement over the mention of new teachers.

Our group has been making bets on what villain Flora turned who is coming to work here. Or maybe it's a princess. We do tend to employ both these days.

Could it be the Little Mermaid, Madame Cleo's bestie?

Or the Ice Queen? Some days, this large, magical castle does get quite warm. Maybe she could cool things down.

Or Hua Mulan? She's supposed to be one of the greatest warriors ever. We could use her. Or Little Red Riding Hood! I think of the bow and arrow she gave me on our quest to find the golden goose, and I grin to myself. Maybe Red is the one who is going to teach our From Mischief-Maker to Model Citizen classes! It makes perfect sense! I smile at Professor Wolfington. I bet he convinced Red to leave the Hollow Woods and teach at Fairy Tale Reform School.

"Without further ado," says Princess Ella in a breathy voice, "the royal court would like to open the doors to Fairy Tale Reform School's new library." Everyone starts to cheer as Ella cuts the ribbon with a large pair of scissors. "It is our hope that the knowledge and dreams you find in the books behind these doors will help you on your journey to not only find yourself, but also to help defend Enchantasia."

Everyone rushes to the doors. I'm not sure most people hear Princess Ella's speech, but it is actually kind of inspiring.

"Ooh!" says the crowd, stopping dead in their tracks as the doors magically open.

Maxine's mouth begins to drool again. "It's like the library goes on forever!"

I squint into the light. Somehow, it feels like the library is actually outdoors on a grassy field. I blink, and the background changes to a snowy mountaintop. I blink again, and I'm standing on a riverbank. Gingerbread, how does the room's view keep changing? And why can't I see a ceiling? Or walls? The floors, however, sparkle like glass, and it's as if the bookcases go on and on forever.

Somewhere in this jungle of books is the one that will give me answers. I just know it.

My friends and I join the slow procession into the library as Miri shouts various instructions from mirrors hanging from stands around the room.

"No touching *any books* until the Magical Librarian arrives! There are rules about these books that must be followed!"

Jocelyn snickers. "Whoever heard of a book having rules? It's not a person."

"No food, drinks, spelling, or wands allowed in the library," Miri adds. "Books are meant to be read, not eaten by your fairy pets! The top floors of the library are for older students only and require permission from the Magical Librarian. First floor only today! No running or flying in the library! And please, keep your voices down!" she yells. Obviously, Miri is exempt from the rules.

"Did you hear that?" I whisper to Jax. "Top floors require permission. That must be where the best books on villains are. Let's go!"

Headmistress Flora steps into my path before I reach the first winding staircase.

"Ms. Cobbler, where do you think you're going? As Miri explained, we are staying on the first floor today."

It's almost as if she knows what I'm after.

"But—" I start to protest.

"Gillian, I told you before," Flora says wearily. "There are days for fighting and days for celebrating, and today is a celebration. Open your eyes and marvel at this place!"

I sigh heavily and let my eyes drift upward. The room is so majestic that I feel like I'm standing in the middle of a royal court palace. There are water fountains with cherub statues that talk and glittering signs that flash to show what books are on which floor. There must be thousands of books in here, shelved on four different floors. The categories fly by: Potions, Spells, Magic Tricks, Hexes, Surviving the High Seas, How to Talk to Animals, and From Wicked to Winning Self-Help Books. I don't see a villain category or the History of Enchantasia section, but they have to be here. A large atrium beckons us forward. It looks so enchanting with all the stained glass windows that seem to reach the school's highest turret. Magic carpets float in the air, waiting to take readers up to out-of-reach shelves, while kids run to cushy, oversize pillows perfect for curling up on for hours of reading, studying, or napping.

Swish! A magic carpet races over my head, carrying books to different shelves. I watch several more zoom past, swooping by a fairy librarian station where workers are reading magical scrolls and wanding books out of thin air.

"Isn't that your sister?" I ask Kayla, pointing out a fairy with shimmery, blue wings on the second floor. The fairy stacks books on a rug that zooms over the atrium to a shelf on another floor.

"Yes, that's Brooke Lynn. My mother and sisters are working in the library," Kayla says proudly.

Kayla seems so much happier now that she has her family back. Her fairy wings have taken on a healthy, glittery appearance, and she's always singing in the hallways. (Thankfully, she has a decent voice.)

"Professor Harlow felt we should all live on school property till we find out what Rumpelstiltskin is up to and what he wanted with my family in the first place."

"They still don't remember anything?" I ask.

Kayla frowns. "No, but they hope having access to the library will help. My mother is a big reader, and she's hoping they'll come across a book that will jog their memories. Mother says our new librarian is the best in all the lands. Not that they'd tell me who she is."

"Greetings, Fairy Tale Reform School students!" a glowing,

white mirror says to a group of kids standing in front of it. "Who can tell the difference between a book you can trust and a book you can't?"

An ogre laughs. "Why wouldn't you trust a book?"

"Well," says the mirror, "it depends who wrote it. Would you trust advice from a villain? What if the villain wrote the book under another name, and you had no idea who the author really was? That's what the librarians are here for. To guide you."

"I don't care what that mirror says. There has to be a section on villains," I tell the others quietly so Flora can't hear me. "We are a school run by former villains, so they must have books about them and where their stories started, don't you think?"

Maxine frowns. "I see a lot of picture books and stories my mother used to tell me in the forest. All these books look safe. Nothing villainous."

They can't all be Mother Goose stories! I scan the spines on the shelf till I find something that looks dark and mysterious. Aha! *The Siren Call of the Deep Sea.* That sounds villainous! Rumpelstiltskin could be mentioned in there. "Look at this one." I glance at the cover. It has gold lettering and a weathered spine that smells a bit like sea air. How can that be? "It has a skull and crossbones on it. Definitely evil!"

"Thief, you're going to get us in trouble," Jax says warily. "We were told not to touch the books till the librarian gets here."

"Don't be such a do-gooder, Prince." Jocelyn takes the book from my hands and feels the raised detail on the cover. "What's the harm in touching a book? I love how wicked this book looks." Her eyes flash darkly. "It's like you can feel the battle between good and evil seeping from the pages." She hugs the book to her chest, and we all look at Jocelyn strangely. "What? Is it wrong to love a good power struggle?"

Ollie quickly takes the book from her. "No, but I think this is a pirate tale."

"Because there is a skull on it?" Jocelyn frowns. "Skulls also stand for poison."

"Or pirates," Ollie counters. He turns the book over in his hands, which are covered with pirate skull and crossbones tattoos he's conjured up.

I can't stand waiting any longer. "Let's take a sneak peek at the first chapter to be sure."

"I think we should wait," Jax says, but I reach over

Ollie and crack the book's spine before anyone can stop me. Immediately, I hear a whooshing sound like wind.

"Uh-oh," Ollie says as Flora and Rapunzel come running from opposite directions.

"Don't open that book any further!" Flora cries, her hands outstretched to snatch it.

Too late. The book jumps from Ollie's hands and spins in the air. The pages blur before the motion stops on an open page. All is quiet.

Ollie sighs. "Oh good. For a minute, I thought—"

His voice is cut off as a pirate leaps out of the pages and points his sword at Maxine's throat.

CHAPTER 2

Time to Duel

Maxine does not appear alarmed by this course of events. "The book came alive!" she says excitedly as the sword presses harder against her wide neck. "The pirate jumped right off the page. Hi, pirate!"

The pirate growls at her, and I yank on Maxine to get her to move. As the pirate charges toward us, water flies from his dirty, ripped clothing, and blood trickles from a fresh cut above his right eye. He looks ghostly, like you could walk right through him, and for a minute, I am sure I'm seeing a mirage, but then he keeps coming.

"Who dares disturb me slumber?" The pirate narrows his eyes at Flora as she finally makes it to our side. "Are ye trying to steal me treasure?"

"No one is stealing your treasure, sir." Flora picks up the book on the floor. "If you would kindly step back inside your story, we can return you to your nap."

The pirate looks around. "Where am I? Where is me ship? I smell sorcery at work." He bares black teeth. "Prepare to duel, me mateys!" He smacks the book out of Flora's hands and a half-dozen pirates spring from the book's pages.

Students dive out of the way as the pirates fan out, slashing their way through the library, poking their swords at bookshelves, and knocking books to the floor. One book flutters open, and a horse pops out. Another book opens, and a flock of birds flies toward the atrium dome.

Rapunzel races toward a pirate who is trying to steal a gold Princess Snow statue off its pedestal. "Someone stop the vagrants!"

"Avast! Stop! Follow the pirate code!" Blackbeard is shouting, but the pirates don't listen. Soon, one is hanging from a chandelier, another is climbing floor to floor, and the others are terrifying students and fairy library workers.

Fiddlesticks. This is all my fault.

I look around for something to stop the first pirate from

hitting Flora or Maxine, but Ollie is way ahead of me. He has his sword out in seconds.

"If it's a fight ye want, it's a fight ye will get!" Ollie races after the pirate heading up the nearest staircase, breaking through the velvet rope that sections it off. The two clash swords, the pirate attempting to push Ollie back down the way he came.

There is a crash behind us. Harlow, Wolfington, and Blackbeard are trying to stop a pirate from pulling a cannon from the pages of a book.

Flora covers her mouth with her hands. "They'll blow the library to bits before our librarian even gets here!" She runs off to help them, leaving Ollie on his own.

"We have to help Ollie," I say to Jax.

"On it!" Jax says. He whistles for Blue, our favorite magic carpet.

The rug zooms over, and I use one of his tassels to pull myself up.

Jax hops on behind me. "Blue, get to Ollie!"

"Don't forget the book!" yells Maxine, tossing it up to me before we fly away.

Kayla flutters alongside us. "Jocelyn and I will corral

the other pirates while you get them back in the book and help Ollie."

"Reform school teamwork," Jax says. "I like it!"

"Hey, pirate? Where are you running?" Jocelyn conjures up a fireball for a pirate threatening a group of kids, sending the pirate running right toward Jax's open book. I hop off Blue and block the pirate's escape route. He's stuck between me, Jocelyn, and Jax. I give him a little kick, and he falls headfirst into Jax's open pages, which suck him back inside.

"Six, seven, eight more to go!" Maxine counts.

"Gillian!" Harlow yells from the floor below. She's whisking several students out of the way of an approaching pirate. "The pirates cannot leave the library! If they get loose..."

Her expression is so dark that I know I don't want to know the end of that sentence.

"Got it!" I shout.

Hearing this, the pirate heads toward the library exit. Jax and I swoop down on him, with Jocelyn aiming another fireball, but this pirate is too quick. Before the fire can singe his trousers, he jumps to a floor below us.

"I could use some help up here!" Ollie shouts.

I look up and spot him sword fighting on a ledge.

"He could fall!" Kayla shrieks. "I'll go spot him!" She flutters up to help him.

"They're going after the princesses!" I hear someone cry.

There are too many of them. Books are falling, kids are crying, and the sound of swords clanging grows louder. Rapunzel is kicking and spinning into pirates, knocking them away from Ella. She's holding her own, but the pirates don't stop. I hear Kayla cry and look up in time to see Ollie almost fall off the ledge.

"We have to get these pirates back in the book *now*," Jax shouts.

"You don't think I know that?" I ask. I whistle loudly. The closest scallywag turns and looks at me. I hold the book out in front of me. "Time to go home!"

The pirate laughs. "We're never going home!"

I narrow my eyes at him. "That's what you think!" I jump off the rug and throw the open book at him, hoping it will grab the pirate and suck him back inside. Instead, the pirate catches the book in one of his filthy hands.

Oops.

"Thanks, Gilly," Jocelyn snaps.

The pirate laughs again. "Foolish lass! You can't beat a pirate!"

He and his friends have the royal court surrounded. One is holding a sword to Ella's neck. Another keeps Jocelyn at bay. Harlow, Kayla, and Ollie are still above us, but for how long? A third pirate has Blackbeard pinned to a wall, and Wolfington is trapped on a floor below. How did the tide turn so quickly?

I have no weapon and my friends are trapped, but I have always liked a challenge.

"Step away from my friends!" I demand.

The pirates all turn toward me. *Gulp.*

"Boys, we'll finish this rug rat first," a pirate says as I start to slowly back away.

Suddenly, there's a roar so loud that it shakes the windows. It sends the birds from the open book into flight and makes fairies hold their pointy ears. But that sound is nothing compared to the sight of a beastly man dropping four stories and landing between me and a band of unruly pirates. The room collectively gasps.

The beast does not waste time. Within seconds, his hairy hands have snatched the pirates' book and opened it to a random page. With another loud roar, he scares a pirate into jumping back inside to avoid his wrath. Then the beast quickly goes after the others, and the same thing happens over and over again.

Freed, we wordlessly move out of the way as the beast runs on all fours after the final pirate, who has escaped to the second level. The beast leaps so high and fast that he outruns the scallywag, cutting him off by a fairy librarian station. There is another ripple of gasps as the beast throws the book at the pirate. That move didn't work for me, but the beast's aim is much better. The book hits the pirate in the face, which sucks him back into his storybook world.

The room is eerily quiet as the beast walks over to the book, picks it up, and holds it securely closed.

"Stay in there!" he roars, his deep, throaty roar reverberating off the walls. His rounded back is rising and falling rapidly as he tries to catch his breath.

The pixie sitting on the shoulder of a goblin next to me topples off in fear.

No one moves. Neither Flora nor Wolfington approach him either, which is why I'm surprised to see a woman rush up to him. She's petite and girlish but obviously older, with long, brown hair piled on her head and the rosiest cheeks I've ever seen. Her dress is golden in color and looks like a tapestry from the walls around us. It's obviously very expensive and yet nothing like the princess dresses I've seen. She hands the beast a small, glittering, blue vial, and he snatches it from her, swallowing it in one gulp.

Maxine hits me so hard that I fall backward into Jax. "Do you know who that is?"

"It's Princess Beauty!" Ollie supplies. "And that must mean that beast is her prince!"

Beauty and the Beast are our new professors at Fairy Tale Reform School?

Even Jocelyn looks stunned.

The beast burps. In the back of the room, I hear a pixie giggle.

The creature whips around to see where the noise came from, and I finally get a good look at him. Oh my Grimm, he's scary! And yet not. He reminds me of Professor Wolfington, who has been known to revert to his wolf side when needed, but this metamorphosis is different. I watch in awe as his hairy face becomes smooth and his long fingernails and horns start to recede. As his body seems to shrink down to normal size, his hair changes to a long, dark mane that frames his pale skin. He blinks big, blue eyes that look more kind than frightening.

"Say hello, darling, or you'll scare them," the woman prompts.

Darling?

The beastly man grunts.

"Darling," she tries again in a singsong voice.

He sighs and rolls his eyes. "Fine! Hello, students!"

His voice is still deep and menacing, but human. A murmur of hellos echoes in the room. Then his face darkens. "First things first: Who was the foolish child who opened that book?"

All eyes in the room are on me. Jax and I make eye contact.

For the love of gingerbread. No one can actually *prove* I was the one who took the book, can they? There are hundreds of people here, and the pirates caused a huge commotion and—

"Girl!" He points to me. "Come here *now*!" His voice makes the stained glass windows shake.

Beauty steps in front of me. She smells like rose petals.

"Darling, that's no way to talk to a student," she says in a wispy voice. "What did I tell you about first impressions?"

"But she could have destroyed the library before you ever

got to use it!" he barks. "And we came all this way! What if Allison Grace had gotten hurt? I told you teaching here wasn't a smart idea!"

Flora clears her throat.

"No offense," he mumbles.

Flora steps forward. "Prince Sebastian, I can assure you, nothing like this will ever happen here again."

Ollie nudges me. "She does remember what school she's talking about, right? Things *always* happen here."

"See?" Beauty rubs the prince's arm. "This is going to be a wondrous adventure for us. Deep breaths in…and out. Try it with me, Seb," she says soothingly.

We watch as he takes several breaths before he calms down. Slowly, his appearance starts to change. He's all man now. A very cranky-looking man giving me the stink eye.

"My apologies for being gruff, but you did open the book without permission," he says.

"Apology accepted, and just so you know, the book opening was an accident," I tell all the adults. "I tripped, and the book popped open."

Ollie coughs. Maxine squirms. Jax runs a hand through his glossy hair. Kayla's wings flutter faster.

What do they want from me? To confess to the royal court, *HEAS*, my old and new professors, *and* the whole school that I almost destroyed the new library? No. Way.

Prince Sebastian narrows his eyes at me. "You tripped?"

He's not buying it.

Beauty steps in. "What's done is done. What's important is that we follow the rules in the future, right?" She looks at me and I nod. "What is your name, child?"

"Gillian." I attempt a curtsy. After all, Beauty is royalty.

"Gillian Cobbler is one of the students who first suggested the new program you will be teaching, Seb," Rapunzel tells him and smiles at me. "She is a clever student."

"*Gillian Cobbler.*" He begins waving his hands around wildly. "Why am I not surprised? Of course you opened the book! You're the reason he's on the run again! You couldn't hold him off in the castle until he could be apprehended, could you? You let him get away!"

I blink rapidly. How does he know about that?

"She's also the reason we got these wonderful new positions," Beauty says graciously.

The prince snorts. "Rumpelstiltskin is out there doing who knows what, and we've had to uproot our lives and pull

Allison Grace away from the safety of home all because of you."

"I don't think he likes you," Jocelyn whispers in my ear. With glee, I might add.

"How are you so familiar with Stiltskin?" I ask curiously.

The prince growls and walks off muttering.

"Professor Wolfington?" Headmistress Flora appeals.

"I'm on it," says my favorite teacher. Maybe they can have a beast-to-beast chat.

"You'll have to excuse him," Beauty tells us. "Stiltskin has also caused much trouble in our kingdom. He's gotten many of our subjects to join his Stiltskin Squad. It's a sore spot with Sebastian since he was unable to stop him. But hopefully now that we're here…"

"Don't worry, B. Our goal is to find him and bring him to justice." Rapunzel puts a hand on Beauty's shoulder. "In the meantime, we're just glad you're here."

"When was the last time we saw you?" Ella asks. "Was it Rose's bachelorette party?"

"Yes, when Rosie got her head stuck in that willow tree on our hike?" Snow says with a laugh.

"Of course!" Beauty says. "We had to send for a flock of

sparrows to peck her out." She shakes her head. "That girl. So headstrong. How is she?"

Ella hesitates slightly. "A few more months at her summer cottage and some work with our fairy godmother Olivina, and she should be as good as new. We hope."

Beauty nods. "A good fairy godmother like Olivina can do anything." They all murmur in agreement.

Professor Harlow clears her throat. "I hate to interrupt such jolly merriment, but, Beauty, maybe you could tell the students a bit about the library before they head to class. This is a school, after all, and we can't stand around all day reminiscing." She gives Beauty a beatific smile that looks semi-sinister to me. The Evil Queen has that effect.

"Oh, of course!" Beauty says. "Raz told me she goes by her first name, so I hope you all will do the same for me. Beauty, or B, is fine," she tells the students. "Sebastian would prefer that you call him Professor, of course. I will send your library class schedules via magical scroll this evening. They will contain library hours as well as policies on taking out books. As you've seen, certain books can only be used in the library." She smiles. "But it's such a lovely space. Why would you want to read anywhere else?"

Certain books can't be checked out? Great! I bet any book on Rumpelstiltskin falls under that category. I raise my hand. "Can we take books out today?" Wilson squeaks in my pocket in agreement.

"Gillian." Headmistress Flora sounds exasperated. "Have you looked around? We have much cleaning up to do before any books can be checked out." She purses her lips. "Or should I say *you* have a lot of cleaning up to do."

"Aye, detention is in order, lass," says Professor Blackbeard. "I'm happy to run this one if you like, Flora, ol' girl."

"Beardie, I told you, we have to go over a few more detention rules before I can allow you to handle some of the detention periods." Madame Cleo giggles. She swims across the mirror in Blackbeard's hand, her mermaid tail glistening silver in the pale-blue waters. Her tail stops swishing. "If only I could remember what those rules are."

"For now, Miss Gillian and her friends who were involved can serve detention in the library by helping clean up," Flora says.

"Why are we in trouble?" Jocelyn complains. "We didn't open the book."

"You didn't stop her either," Flora reminds her. "You'll all help Gillian clean up."

"They can't do it alone," says Beauty. "This collection has some unique books that have to be handled delicately." Her brown eyes light up. "But my daughter, Allison Grace, knows these books well and can help you. Allison?" She looks around. "Where are you, dear?"

A girl slightly younger than me steps slowly out of the crowd, her head bent so low that her brown, curly hair covers her face. She's wearing a fluffy, pink gown with shiny gold shoes with tiny butterfly clips on them. Anna always wanted Father to make her shoes just like them. When the girl looks up, I suck in my breath. She even looks like Anna. Allison Grace stares at me shyly, and I feel a pang in my chest. I miss Anna so much that it hurts.

"This is Allison Grace," Beauty tells us. "She's going to be a new student at FTRS." Beauty pulls Allison Grace's hair off her face. I watch the girl move closer to her mother.

"If she's royal, why isn't she going to Royal Academy with the other royals?"

Of course that question comes from Tessa, our Royal Ladies-in-Waiting leader, who is eyeing Allison Grace with interest.

"If she went to RA like I once did, she'd be away from

us." Beauty hugs her daughter. "Our family agreed that keeping her close is for the best."

"If Father had his way, I'd be homeschooled," Allison Grace murmurs, and I'm the only one who laughs. She looks at me, and we share a smile. I can't get over how much she looks like my sister. Is anyone else noticing the resemblance?

"You were homeschooled before," the prince says, walking back over with Professor Wolfington. "I don't see what's so bad about continuing the same schooling in Enchantasia." He looks at Flora. "Allison isn't one for crowds."

"*Father*," the girl whispers, her face heating up.

"Which is why it will be wonderful for Allison Grace to take smaller classes, like the one you're teaching," Beauty says reassuringly. "Allison Grace is excited, aren't you?"

"I guess." She avoids looking at any of us.

"Sheltered much?" Jocelyn asks us.

Jax shrugs. "It happens sometimes. When you're royal, you're alone in a castle so much that sometimes you can't relate to anyone outside those walls. Another reason I'm glad I go here."

Our conversation is interrupted by the sound of a loud foghorn.

Blackbeard cheers. "Jolly roger, it's working! Much better than chimes, eh, Flora?"

"*That's* the new sentencing alarm?" Harlow looks livid. "I thought we decided on claps of thunder. These children coming in need to know we mean business!"

"I wanted a lovely wind-chime sound." Madame Cleo sighs. "We don't want to scare them off."

The professors start bickering, and Miri interrupts.

"Headmistress?" The nearest mirror glows red and pink. "We have an emergency sentencing that Pete would like you to handle right away."

"*Now?*" Headmistress Flora sighs and claps her hands to get the room's attention. Kids look up from the bookstacks, reading nooks, and library information centers. "Children, you are dismissed and should go to class. There will be time to explore the library later."

A collective groan is uttered at the word *class*.

It's followed by what sounds like a roar. I see Beauty nudge her husband.

My friends and I use the ensuing mass exit chaos as a

distraction to try to get out of our punishment. Harlow points a red fingernail in our direction when she sees us slinking out.

"Uh-uh. Not you all," she says, her lips pulling into a tight smile. "You're on cleanup duty. Wait here. The elf cleaning crew will get you some cleanup tools."

"Thanks a lot, Cobbler." Jocelyn drops onto a feather bag chair.

I sit down beside her and watch the students file out, along with the royal court and the reporter from *HEAS* who is still asking questions. Beauty and the prince are talking quietly with their daughter on their way out the door. I can't hear what they're saying, but suddenly, Allison Grace laughs and hugs both her parents. I feel a small pang, knowing my own sister isn't around to do the same thing.

Pete and Olaf burst into the library, each holding the arm of a curly-haired boy whose mocha skin is covered in what looks like flour. I don't recognize him. Pete pushes the boy into the center of the room and throws his hands up.

"This one needs maximum security! He's only been in the village a week, and he's already… He's… He's… Three times! One week! The flour factory, the Three Little Pigs, and… He's got to go here even without any parent permission. I insist."

I haven't heard Pete this flustered since he apprehended…me.

Flora reaches for the scroll that contains the boy's rap sheet. "Caught stealing rolls from Gnome-olia Bakery on Monday afternoon."

"I was hungry, okay?" The boy looks up at Flora with big, brown eyes. "So were some of the other kids on the street." His mouth tightens. "I'd do it again if I could."

"Same as me," I whisper to Jax. "I used to steal bags of rolls for my family from there all the time."

Flora keeps reading. "Two days later, you were caught pinching clothes from Combing the Sea."

"I stole from there too!" I nudge Jax again. That's where I got Anna's dragon-tooth comb.

The boy hangs his head. "I've been in the same rags for weeks, okay? Besides, I didn't just steal them for me. I was looking for a gift for my mum."

"And then today, you were caught stealing a rib-eye steak from the Dwarf Police Squad Annual Picnic."

Now that's something I haven't done.

"I'd marinated that steak for days!" Pete rails. "Finest piece of meat this side of the kingdom! Ordered it weeks ago for the party! Olaf and I couldn't wait to dive into it, and this kid stole it right off the grill and tossed it in the trash!" He glares at the boy in his possession.

"You shouldn't eat meat," the kid says. "Cows have feelings too, you know. My cow, Milky Way, is my best friend." He looks down again. "Or at least he was, till Rumpelstiltskin stole him and my mum. I've been on my own ever since."

I feel a pang of sadness mixed with anger for this boy whose life seems to mirror my own. He's alone because of Stiltskin. I'm without Anna for the same reason. I step forward to speak up, but Wolfington cuts in.

"In Enchantasia, putting your worst foot forward has consequences. What's your name, boy?"

The kid looks Wolfington straight in the eye. "Jack Spriggins."

"Jack Spriggins? You're the one who climbed the beanstalk!" Maxine cries. There is a murmur among the staff and my friends.

This boy is *the* Jack? My brothers and sisters loved hearing Jack's story when Father would tell it at bedtime. He told it so often that my siblings memorized it. I rack my brain thinking of the key details. Beanstalk, giant, golden egg, huge reward. But if that's true, why is Jack still stealing?

"That was just a bedtime story," Jax says. "There's no such thing as a city at the top of a beanstalk."

"Tell that to the giant who fell in my yard," Jack fires back, and the two narrow their eyes at each other. "There are giants up there and treasures like you've never seen."

"And yet you're stealing bread," Jax reminds him.

"*Jax*," I whisper. He's being rude.

Jack continues to look at Jax. I mean Jack. I mean Jax! Wow, this is going to be confusing. "You have no idea what I've been through, Prince," Jack says. "Tangoing with Rumpelstiltskin and then getting away is no picnic."

My ears perk up. "You've seen him? When?"

He shrugs. "I can't remember. It all happened so fast."

"He's telling tales again. And how do you know I'm a prince anyway?" Jax counters.

Jack looks him up and down. "I can tell."

"Enough shop talk," says Pete, leading Jack away. "Let's get you signed in, Spriggins."

I watch Pete lead Jack away and wish I could go after them. I have to know more about what happened between him and Rumpelstiltskin!

Happily Ever After Scrolls

Brought to you by Fairy Web—Enchantasia's

Number One News Source!

Meet the Beast: Fairy Tale Reform School Has a New Teacher—Prince Sebastian!

by Coco Collette

Name: Prince Sebastian, but you may know him best as the royal who was once cursed to live out his days as a beast. Then true love's kiss by a young maiden named Beauty changed his fate!

Occupation: In his own kingdom, the prince ruled the countryside with the help of his princess and their young daughter, Allison Grace, who is reportedly attending Fairy Tale Reform School. As a princess, we wondered why she wasn't enrolled at Royal Academy. "That's none of your business," said Prince Sebastian gruffly. (Geez, guess some of that beast is still in him. When he gets cranky, sources say he turns back into one too! Let's not make him angry, okay?) At FTRS, the prince will be handling the school's new advanced studies program for students already on the path to being good, nicknamed the MMC. "My goal is to keep them that way," the prince says. His coursework aims to help the students find a deeper understanding of themselves and the kingdom around them.

Hobbies: Literature. Like his wife, he's a huge lover of books. The prince also loves to travel. "Once I was freed of my curse, I wanted to explore places outside my castle. There's no greater joy than experiencing other kingdoms and seeing how they differ from your own courtyard."

Strengths: Um, actual strength? When he's in beast form, he can scale walls and lift heavy objects. Another strength? "My family," says the prince, who credits his wife and daughter for making him "worthy of the man I see in the mirror." Aww!

Weaknesses: "I'm grumpy when I'm hungry. And when someone doesn't listen to the rules. And when I'm contradicted." (Note to us all: do not make him angry!)

Check back soon for our Meet the Teacher report on the prince's wife—Beauty!

CHAPTER 3

Into the Woods

Even though I went to bed hours ago, I still can't sleep. My mind is on my first class with Prince Sebastian. These classes were my idea, so I want to make a good impression. Especially, um, after what happened in the library.

Tomorrow, I will arrive early!

My quill will be full of ink, and my scroll will be ready for note taking!

My uniform is going to be pressed, and my hair is going to be neatly tied back in a ribbon!

Do I have any hair ribbons? I keep losing the ones Maxine gives me. I will need to ask Maxine for another ribbon.

I toss and turn and almost knock Wilson off my pillow three times while Maxine and Peaches snore loudly together from the other bed. A duck snore is not a pretty sound. I cover my ears—and hear my name called.

"Gilly!" Kayla is banging on Maxine's and my bedroom window. I can see her fluttering outside it. "I need your help!"

I glance at our newest alarm clock—Peaches keeps eating them because she hates the noise—and almost pass out. It's 1:00 a.m.? How can I still be awake?

"Gilly, please!" Her voice is desperate. It's the Kayla of old, and I really like the new, happy Kayla. "It's Mother." She sounds frantic. "She's missing from the fairy hut, and I'm worried he'll find her if she's out on the grounds alone!"

I know the "he" she is referring to. I get out of bed, slip into my boots, and run to the window in my nightgown. To avoid tripping the magical alarm that will alert Miri that I'm out of bed after curfew, I have to make my exit quick. We are on a low floor, but still high enough that I can't jump. I'll have to spring off Maxine's super-springy ottoman, through the window, and into Kayla's arms.

I take a deep breath and listen to Maxine's snoring. "Ready?" I whisper.

"Ready!" Kayla whispers, reaching her arms out to catch me.

This isn't the first time we've done this move.

I hit the ottoman and fly through the window into Kayla's arms. She catches me, and we both listen closely for a second, neither of us moving. Nope, no alarm. We are clear! Kayla flies me to the edge of the woods where her family's hut is, quickly explaining to me what happened.

"My sisters are away overnight, taking a fairy librarian course with Beauty—it's their first time away since they've become fairies again. I said I'd keep an eye on Mother, but I didn't know that *literally* meant 'keep an eye on her.' I put her to bed, but when I checked on her a little while ago, she was gone!"

The cool night air we are flying through makes my eyes water. "Did she say she wanted to go out before bed?" We land near a patch of trees.

"She kept asking me for 'the book' at dinner." Kayla makes air quotes. "She's been talking about books a lot since she started working at the library, but this was different. She says this book is calling to her." Kayla's eyes shine in the glow of the moonlight. "Gilly, I think something's wrong with her."

"I'm sure she's just confused," I say, trying to sound sure although this does sound strange. What is Kayla's mom talking about? I know she's been a little off since her transformation, but I didn't know she was mumbling about books. I search behind a patch of sunflowers that are moving, but all I find is a family of bunnies. The hair stands up on my arms. What if Kayla's mom really was kidnapped by Stiltskin? "How long ago did you check on her?" I can't let Kayla know I'm panicking.

"Like an hour ago!" Kayla cries. "She was still muttering about the book, so I said we could take it out of the library tomorrow. She got all excited, and I thought that was the end of it. But then she was gone. I checked the library first, but it's empty. Where could she be?" Kayla sits down on a tree stump and covers her face with her hands. "I'm going to have to wake Flora or Harlow, aren't I? Harlow will kill me! You know how the Evil Queen feels if she doesn't get eight solid hours of beauty sleep!"

Kayla is so busy freaking out that I think I am hearing things, but the sound grows louder. Someone is mumbling. I shush Kayla and spin around, listening closely. I hear the rustling of wind, the trees, an owl in the distance, and then—a voice!

"This way!" I head into a patch of trees. We're close to

the edge of the Hollow Woods now and have to be careful (especially at night). But the voice is close. If I just go a little farther…I round one more bend, and that's when I see Kayla's mom sitting on a rock talking to herself.

"Mother!" Kayla rushes toward her as a wolf howls in the distance. "What are you doing out here?" She pulls off her jacket and wraps it around her mother, who is wearing a thin nightgown.

Kayla's mom looks up at her with wild amber eyes. "The book called to me! I came to find it, but it's not here. It's never here. I have to find it first! I have to find it first. I have to find it first," she repeats as she looks around the forest. "Where are you! I hear you, but I can't see you!" she shouts.

"Shh!" Kayla and I say. I worry we'll wake a sleeping giant or, worse, a sleeping Harlow.

"We'll get it at the library tomorrow, but tonight you need sleep," Kayla says soothingly. She mouths *thank you*, and we try to bring her mother back to the fairy hut.

"No!" Kayla's mom pulls away. "You don't understand! I have to get to it first. It's mine to protect, and I've lost it. I have to find it before they do, or all will be lost." She appears frightened. "If they get their hands on it, they'll know what to do and Enchantasia will be lost."

I feel a shiver in my nightdress and tell myself it's just the wind giving me goose bumps.

"Don't worry. I've seen the book and it's safe," I say to help things along.

Kayla's mom's face lights up. "You have it? It's safe? Take me to it!"

"In the morning," I promise, and Kayla smiles at me gratefully. We both steer her mother successfully out of the edge of the woods and toward their hut. "But only if you wait till morning."

"Okay," her mom promises, yawning. The sound makes Kayla and me yawn too. "In the morning."

I'm sure she'll forget about this book by then.

CHAPTER 4

From Mischief Makers to Model Citizens

Q*uack!*

Quack!

Squeak!

I wake up to animals pecking and scratching my bare legs. I sit straight up, wincing as the sunlight streams through our bedroom window, and stare blearily at Peaches and Wilson.

"What time is it?" I ask the fairy pets as if they can answer.

I hear a chime, and then a wooden voice says, "The time is now 10:15 a.m. Maxine tried to get you up three times! You are late! Late for an important date!"

I look in horror at the rabbit-shaped alarm clock holding a pocket watch, and I have two thoughts.

When did we get a talking alarm clock?

How does it know I'm late? *Gasp!* I'm late for my first class with Prince Sebastian!

I jump out of bed in a frenzy. I throw my wrinkled jumper on over my nightdress before slipping into my boots without my striped stockings. There's no time to tame my hair. I grab my half-empty quill and scroll before dashing out of my dorm room. So much for looking presentable.

"No running in the hallways, Gilly!" Miri shouts as I fly down the stairs and through hallways, trying to find the new library services wing. "Detention, Gilly! Did you hear me? That's two detentions! Gilly? Gilly!"

But I ignore Miri and keep running, barely missing a gaggle of pixies chatting in the hall.

"Blackbeard's class is on the first floor!" I say as I dive through an opening hallway and fly into the library services wing. I keep running past the stained glass windows and don't stop till I find the door that says PRINCE SEBASTIAN'S CLASSROOM. I pound on the door.

I fail to see the fine print till afterward. IF THE DOOR IS SHUT, CLASS IS ALREADY IN SESSION AND YOU ARE LATE! DON'T BOTHER!

Fiddlesticks.

The door to my new classroom flies open.

"You're late!" Prince Sebastian growls. His long hair is tied back with a red ribbon, and he's wearing a red jacket with gold buttons. He looks at my disheveled appearance with disdain.

"Sorry, I know," I say fast. "My alarm clock didn't go off and I was busy helping a friend last night and I overslept and didn't have time to iron and it won't happen again."

The prince is breathing heavily as he stares at me. I wait for him to beast out, but he just turns and walks away. "This is your first and only warning about being late to my class. Next time, you won't be allowed entrance."

"Prince Sebastian?" Miri glows in a nearby mirror, and I cringe. "Headmistress Flora would like a word."

"Of course," says the prince. "Gillian, sit! And the rest of you, keep quiet until I return."

"Thank you, Professor," I say as he leaves the room. "I'll just sit down...oh!"

This is strange. There are no desks in the classroom. I spot my friends all seated at individual dressing tables that have their own gold mirrors, chandeliers, and gold rugs beneath their feet. Classical music is playing from a harp in the corner and… What's that smell? Lavender incense? I slide behind an open vanity across from someone I didn't expect to see—Allison Grace. While everyone else talks quietly with the person nearest them, Beauty and the Beast's daughter is wringing her hands, tapping her toes, and looking everywhere but at me. Being the new kid can be rough.

"Hey, Allison Grace," I say, tripping over her formal name. "Do you go by both names all the time? Or just Allison? Or maybe Grace?" She looks at me strangely. "It takes so long to say both names, you know?"

"My parents love my name, but…" She sighs and puts her hands firmly on the desk. "It sounds so formal, like I'm being announced at a ball. All. The. Time."

I laugh. "How about a nickname for school?"

She looks thoughtful. "I've never had a nickname before."

"The easier it is to say your name, the more likely it is that kids will call it out," I tell her.

Her face lights up. "What would my nickname be?"

I think for a moment. "Ali? Ali Grace? Gracey?" She wrinkles her nose at each suggestion. "How about AG?"

"AG?" Allison Grace repeats, and her smile widens. "I love it! Now how do I get people to use it?"

"Easy!" I whistle, and everyone turns around. "You guys remember meeting Allison Grace in the library?" People nod. "Well, from here on out, she'd love for you to call her AG."

A chorus of "Hey, AG!" rings out around the room, and my new friend looks tickled pink. I wink at her as someone slides into the seat behind her. It's Jack Spriggins.

"How'd you get in this class?" Jocelyn asks pointedly. "Weren't you just sentenced?"

Jack shrugs. "Don't know. The headmistress said my story reminded her of hers." He points to me.

"Gilly?" Jax sputters. "You're nothing like her."

Jack narrows his eyes at my princely friend. "That's not what the headmistress thinks. And hey—who am I to argue? I saw the class list. I'll take this class over Suppressing the Villain Within any day."

"Good point," I agree, and Jax looks at me.

Maybe I'm getting soft, but I feel bad for Jack. We seem to have some things in common. As the others turn back to their conversations, I can't help but say what's been on my mind since yesterday. "I'm sorry about your mom...and, um, cow."

Jack's brown eyes look sad, and yet he says, "I don't need your pity."

"Who said pity?" I stiffen. "I'm just saying I get it. Stiltskin took someone I love. Is that what happened to your family?"

Jack is quiet for a moment. "Yes." He moves his chair closer to mine. "Did you get the people you lost back?"

"No." My voice breaks. "My sister went with him a few months ago. She hasn't returned."

Jack's mouth falls open, and I fear the fly buzzing around Maxine will land on his tongue. "My mum and cow were taken. But your sister *willingly* joined the Stiltskin Squad?"

"Yes." I feel pained even talking about this. "She felt like Stiltskin understood her in a way we didn't. We haven't heard from her since. I know the professors and the royal court are on the case, trying to find all the missing kids. They say they'll track him down, but…it's taking forever."

He laughs. "You think that royal court of yours is going to get the job done? All they care about are their crowns. They don't care about your sister or my mum."

I blink.

"I'm not sitting here waiting for someone else to do

something they're just going to screw up." Jack looks around carefully. "First chance I get, I'm breaking out of here and finding my mum and Milky Way."

I snort. "Good luck with that. Students never break out of FTRS. You'll get caught."

There is a glint in his eye I recognize well. "That doesn't mean I can't try." His voice softens, and he stares into his vanity mirror as if it contains all the answers. "I'm all they've got in this world. The longer my mum and cow are with Stiltskin, the better the chance he can control them and keep them with him for good."

I shudder. "You think he's brainwashed your family?"

"My mum and cow don't have an evil bone in their bodies," Jack explains. "But the longer people are around Stiltskin, the more they start to think like him, you know? How else do you think he gets so many people to turn evil?"

Anna? Evil? Never... I hope. She'll come to her senses and leave his squad soon. I know she will.

"He's coming!" someone whispers.

Everyone quickly gets back to their seats as the prince enters the room with a purposeful stride. "My apologies. Let's begin the class that will transform your little lives."

I want to give a sarcastic reply, but I am on thin ice as it is, so I keep my mouth shut. I want this class to go well. I can only imagine what we'll be learning in here. Will it be hands-on, like Red was in the Hollow Woods? Or will we be taking lots of field trips to the village to watch different businesses at work? Is the prince going to bring in experts to tell us about different fields? Or will we be required to shadow workers to get a feel for their responsibilities? I'm so excited, I can't stop bouncing in my seat, even if there is a silly mirror in front of me. What's this about? I wonder if Miri is watching us to make sure we behave for our newest teacher.

The prince snaps his fingers, and gold quills appear on our desks. "We will start today's class by writing down the class rules."

Boring!

Scrolls appear in front of us. "From Mischief Makers to Model Citizens is a new program, and the headmistress and I will be constantly revising and reviewing our plans for the syllabus. Eventually we will have a full schedule that will replace all your other classes, but for now you will take this class in addition to the rest of your regular coursework." We all moan, and the prince grunts in a beastly manner. "Be grateful you only have one class with me right now. Write this down." We grab our quills. "You will arrive to class, not on time, but *early*. We have much to cover and not a lot of time to do it. You will have weekly assignments in addition to larger projects that you will have several months to complete. You must receive a B plus or higher on all assignments for you to stay in this line of classes."

"B plus?" I can't help but ask. "It's a C in our other classes." AG's toes start tapping again.

"Yeah, seems extreme when you aren't even sure what the coursework is yet," chimes in Jack.

Prince Sebastian leans closer to the two of us, his blue eyes blazing. "This isn't like other classes. I expect both discipline and excellence. Being good isn't enough. You must be great. To assure that, the headmistress and I have a system in place. If your grades fall below a B plus three times, you will be dropped from this class."

"Dropped?" Maxine's mouth opens wide. The prince closes it.

"No one said growth was easy. It takes discipline. Complete your work and your assignments to my standards, and this won't be an issue. Get sloppy, and you'll regret it.

Once you're dropped from this class, you'll need to reapply and there is already a wait list."

I feel myself growing angrier. I could get kicked out of the class *I* suggested? I don't think so. Who does this prince think he is?

Prince Sebastian snaps his fingers, and an hourglass appears on each of our desks. "Time waits for no man. You want to succeed in Enchantasia and make something of yourself? You will need to work harder than the children in the village and the students at Royal Academy. You will have to be more gracious than royals. You need to be two steps ahead of everyone around you. Why? Because you have a stigma on your back that royals and regular villagers do not. You are former villains—or were on the path to becoming ones—so you have reputations that it could take a lifetime to repute."

"A reputation?" I scoff. I can't help myself. He's acting like he's doing us a favor by being here. We got him this gig. "We're here because we're heroes. I don't know if you've heard much about this group, but we've already been pardoned for doing good. We saved this school and rid it of Stiltskin. Our reputations can't be beat."

"You're arrogant and smug," the prince says bluntly. Jocelyn snickers. "Those are not characteristics of a future leader. Hero or no hero, people quickly forget past accomplishments. They want to know what you are doing *now*. However, what they never forget are manners, intelligence, and a strong sense of self. Someone who holds himself or herself in high esteem but gives back to those around them is someone who will go far in life. I was arrogant, selfish, and vain once," he says softly. "That cost me many years of my life. I had to think about what was best for those around me before I could change myself." He stands up straighter and looks at us. "So today's assignment is: Who are you?"

The mirrors in front of us begin to glow.

"I want you to look deep into the mirror and write what you see on your scroll. Who is the person staring back at you? Do you like what you see? Who does this person want to become? What are their dreams? Hopes? What do they want to accomplish?"

I have no clue who I want to be! That's why I'm in this class! That's why we're all in this class! None of us know who we want to... I look around. *Oh*.

Ollie is scribbling furiously. So are Jax, Kayla, and AG.

Even Jocelyn is writing in big, loopy scrolls. Jack taps his quill against his desk and winks at me. His scroll is blank. At least someone is in the same boat as me.

The prince coughs. "These will be graded, so please think before you use your quill. You have twenty minutes to gather your thoughts. Then we will discuss the first big assignment that you will need to work on outside of class."

Holy gingerbread, this guy moves fast! Shouldn't the first day of class be all about him and what we'll be learning? Instead, the prince is giving us big speeches and homework. I narrow my eyes at him as he walks over to Maxine, whose hand is raised. He speaks to her in hushed tones, and she smiles gratefully. I bet he doesn't even know what this class is going to be about yet.

"Do your work," Jax whispers to me.

I turn and stare at myself in the mirror. What do I see?

A girl who hates pointless assignments.

A girl who can't get rid of that purple stripe in her hair no matter how many spells she tries. (Jocelyn swears there is no way to undo it.)

A girl who hates her school uniform but hated life without it.

A girl who is really glad there's not an RLW meeting today, or she'd have to describe her garish pink sash.

A girl who only wears one pair of boots because they're broken in, good for outrunning danger, and the only pair of shoes she'll ever need. (Father made them so they're built to last.)

But I can't write any of these things because I know what the prince will say: those are superficial answers. They don't explain who I am. I'd just be describing my appearance, and I've never cared about that. Anna was the one into lotions and hair care and smelling sweet. She was always trying to spritz me with some new perfume she'd concocted.

But that was before, when she was good. Before I somehow made her feel like nothing she had was hers alone. Before I somehow pushed her to choose evil. How can I be a good person when I turned my own sister to villainy? My heart hurts, thinking about Anna. I can't believe that she really wants to be working with Stiltskin. Does she still? I think about what Jack said earlier. What if Anna wants to come home and can't?

With a loud groan, I look around. How long have I been sitting here worrying about Anna instead of myself? My friends are all writing furiously. Maxine is writing so much, she keeps dipping her quill in the ink jar. The room is so quiet I could hear a pin drop. The prince is sitting at his own desk reading a history book. I better look away before he looks up. Even Jocelyn is scribbling away. What is she writing? I try to lean over to see.

Boom! I lean a little too far and fall off my chair, banging into my table and knocking the mirror off the desk. It smashes to the ground and shatters. The sound echoes through the room.

The prince walks over. "Time," he says flatly, picking up my parchment, which is empty. "I guess there is no need to grade this, Miss Gillian. As I expected, an F. That's your first demerit."

"What? No!" I protest.

"Give her a break, Teach. It's our first class," Jack says, and the prince glares at him so hard he shuts up.

"Yelling and complaining won't get you anywhere in life. Believe me, I've tried. You must do the work." The prince walks away to collect the other parchments.

My chest is rising and falling heavily. I've failed my first assignment! He can't grade me on an assignment I wasn't even prepared to write. Maybe I can talk to Flora or Rapunzel. I won't accept an F from a class I suggested!

"Your first in-depth assignment will be due in three weeks," the prince tells us. "It is a family tree project."

That sounds easy enough. I could do one of those in my sleep. Instant A.

"But this is no simple family tree." The prince seems to hear my thoughts. "I want you to not only research who you are and how you are connected to this kingdom but also interview your family members about their feelings toward you and each other. Think of it as a mini-biography on each family member that explores your difficulties and triumphs with them. How have they impacted your life, and how have you impacted theirs? You should also include personal magical photos and any trinkets that speak to your family's history in Enchantasia."

No. My heart starts to beat faster. I don't want to talk about what happened with Anna or how it's torn our family apart.

"What if some of your family members were killed in the Troll War?" Maxine asks.

"Or they were kidnapped by an evil villain?" Jack adds.

"We will discuss any difficulties about completing the

assignment in private," the prince says, "but if the person is living, they must be interviewed, and if they can't be, then you must interview those who know them best about their relationship to you."

I can't do it.

The prince paces the room. "Before I dismiss you, there is one more thing we need to discuss: your freedom. As you are advancing to tougher coursework, we feel you are mature enough for privileges regular students cannot have, and that includes going home to visit your families once a month." The prince looks at me. "As long as your coursework is exemplary."

I'm going to growl like a beast myself if he doesn't let up on me.

"That is all. Class dismissed."

I grab my books from the floor and follow my friends out.

"Well, that was fun," I say sarcastically. "The prince is great."

"Isn't he?" Maxine says dreamily, drool dripping onto her school uniform. "He gave me such a good pep talk about beauty being found within that I wrote three pages of scroll-work! I'm sure I got an A." She drifts off happily as I stare after her.

At least *someone* is killing it with our new teacher.

Hello, darling!

We received the scroll from Headmistress Flora telling us about the new program that you've been accepted into. We are so proud of you! Your brothers and sisters are so excited you will be able to come home to visit some weekends.

We also received the Evil Queen's—I mean, Professor Harlow's—antidote to Mr. Stiltskin's muffins. Goodness, how could we have been so easily fooled by that man? You were wise to avoid eating one (even if they were delicious. I wonder what he used to make them taste like toffee. Caramel, perhaps? Anyway...). Your father and I wanted you to know that we're so sorry we doubted you. While Father and many in the village continue to search for Mr. Stiltskin and the missing children, they seem to have disappeared without a trace. And yet, just when we thought all hope was lost, we received a scroll from Anna this week! She says she's fine and having a grand adventure with her new friends. There was no return address. I'm sad she hasn't come home yet, but I am sure she will turn herself around when she's ready. After all, you did.

Love,
Mother

CHAPTER 5

Walk on the Wild Side

ᴕᴕ

Maxine reads over the Pegasus Post I just received and has the same reaction I did. "Anna wrote your mother and not you? She can't still be mad at you, can she?"

"I guess she still is," I say, feeling embarrassed. Then a thought occurs to me. "Unless she didn't write that scroll."

"What do you mean?" Maxine asks.

"Why would she send my parents a scroll claiming how happy she is to be on some big adventure?" I question. "Anna never liked to brag. Maybe Stiltskin wrote that scroll to keep us off the scent because he doesn't want Anna to leave the squad." I think of what Jack said about his mum and cow being around the troll for too long. "How could she still think he's better than sliced cheese?" I say to myself as much as to Maxine.

"There's no way she thinks he's as good as sliced cheese." Maxine nods her head vigorously. "That is like the best food invention ever! Stiltskin can't compare to that." Drool drips down her chin. "But *if* she did write that scroll, she's obviously happy that she went with Stiltskin, and I don't think she's coming back anytime soon."

I take back the scroll. "I know." I stare at a group of trolls carrying swords on their way to early-morning pirate training with Blackbeard. They're all wearing eye patches and bumping into walls. Alongside them, a group of mermaids swims swiftly by behind one of the clear glass walls. Suddenly, they stop as a new hallway waffles in front of us and changes our direction. Jax and Ollie come rolling out of it.

"Aye, it's a beautiful morning!" says Ollie, walking proudly with his RLW sash prominently placed over his uniform.

"You know we don't have a meeting today, right?" I ask him.

Ollie gives me a look. "A good RLW wears his sash with pride every day of the week."

"Show-off," I mumble.

"Who sent a Pegasus Post?" asks Jax, pointing to the scroll in my hand.

"Anna!" Maxine can't contain herself. "To Gilly's mom,

and she claims she's happy she left town with the Stiltskin Squad and is basically living on a rainbow." She pauses. "Okay the last part is an exaggeration."

Jax looks at me, his violet eyes shimmering. "There is no way Anna wrote that scroll."

"Thank you!" I throw my hands up. "I know she wanted to be in the Stiltskin Squad, but by now she must realize he's up to no good, right?"

Jocelyn appears out of nowhere and steals the scroll. She and Kayla, who has fluttered over, read it quickly. "Not if she's meant to be evil," Jocelyn says. "Evil likes evil, remember?"

"My sister is not evil," I say firmly. "She's just confused." I look at the scroll again. "*I think*."

Ollie peeks at the scroll. "She doesn't *sound* confused. It sounds like she loves traveling, and your mom thinks she's having a good time."

"Mothers always want to believe the best of their kids," Jocelyn says. "So I've heard."

"Mother would feel better knowing Anna isn't in trouble, but Anna has been gone for two months. Why send Mother a Pegasus Post now? It's like she wants to send me a message."

"She might be." Jax adjusts his school uniform shirt,

positioning the new-and-improved crest (which now includes a skull and crossbones for Blackbeard and a rose for Beauty and the Beast) over his heart. "Raz just got word from the royal guards that there are over a hundred children from our kingdom and neighboring ones working for the Stiltskin Squad now. If he's getting kids to join him willingly, he's spinning quite the tall tale. Anna is either telling the truth about enjoying his crew or trying to let you know she's in trouble." He frowns. "I'm just not sure which it is."

I try to ignore the worried feeling gnawing at me.

"New hall!" Ollie shouts as a scrolled archway shimmers before appearing a few feet from us. We break into a run to reach it before it disappears. Jax and I are the last ones through. I slide into the hallway as it closes, landing on my back. I look up and see a giant, gray foot coming down on my stomach.

Jax pulls me away before the foot hits the ground with a thunderous shake.

"Sorry, Gilly!" says Millie, a goblin I know from the RLWs. "Teensy needed a walk before Magical Fairy Pets class, and I got lost."

Teensy is a full-size elephant that is about to charge down a hallway full of students.

"Ms. Millie!" Headmistress Flora hurries through a doorway that opens behind us. "What have I told you about bringing Teensy through the halls? Always use the *outside* entrance for large animals." The headmistress waves a wand, and a doorway to the yard outside our classroom opens up. Millie leads Teensy outside. A baby giraffe and a cow are already grazing in the gated area. The cow makes me think of Jack again. I wonder if he's in this class.

"Come in, children," says Flora, motioning to the door to her left, which has recently been patched after an ostrich pecked its way to freedom. "Class starts in ten minutes."

I didn't think Flora would keep teaching after regaining her title as headmistress, but I guess she doesn't mind being pooped on a few days a week. I slip into my seat in the second row and pull Winston out of my pocket, resting him in a tiny pen on my desk. I plunk a small piece of cheddar cheese that I saved from last night's dinner in the pen with him to nibble on. He squeaks gratefully. I wink back at him as a symphony of neighs, baas, tweets, barks, and other sounds take over the room. Ollie's parrot is sitting on his shoulder, while Jax's dog is doing flips on his desk.

"*Quack!*"

Peaches swoops over my desk and swallows Winston's cheese in one gulp. Winston immediately starts yelling at her. Peaches quacks back.

"Maxine! Would you please keep Peaches on a leash in here?" I push the duck away, and it nips at me. "She can't eat everything in sight!"

Maxine gently pulls Peaches back to her desk and puts the duck on her oversize chair next to her. "Peaches hates the leash." Maxine frowns. "She ate the last two I bought her."

"Well, you have to do something," I say as the goose coughs up a pencil.

"Oh good, I needed one of those," Maxine says. "Thanks, Peaches!" She pats the goose's head.

"The cafeteria is right down the hall," I tell Winston. "I'll be there and back with more cheese before class starts."

I slip out the door without Flora noticing and follow the scent of tomato bisque down the hall. As I hoped, I'm able to run into the cafeteria and grab cheese without anyone noticing. I'm almost back to class when I spot Jack outside the Fairy Pets classroom. For some reason, I slow up so he can't see me. He's talking to someone… Wait. It's some*thing*. I step closer. A mirror? Jack spins around.

"What are you doing?" I ask, looking at him strangely.

Jack hides the gold mirror behind his back sheepishly. "Nothing! I'm on my way to Magical Fairy Pets and I-I…" I walk closer. "Okay, you caught me." He pulls the mirror back out. "I was giving myself a pep talk. I've been doing it every morning since I got here." He looks into the mirror again. "Hey, you. You're going to do great today and find your mum before you know it. Stay strong." He looks at me worriedly.

I want to laugh, but it's not such a bad idea. Jack doesn't know anyone here. Why would he trust anyone other than himself?

"Do not tell the others," he begs. "Please?"

"Your secret is safe with me," I say as the bell rings. "But you better hide that mirror before class."

Jack slides it into his pants pocket, and the two of us run into class. He takes the first seat he finds, and I head to the back as Jax watches me curiously. I place the piece of cheese in front of Winston, and he squeaks happily.

"Guard it with your life," I whisper.

"Today we are going to continue to work on teaching our fairy pets to obey commands using the reward system," says

Flora, tapping the board with her wand. A list of instructions glimmers and glows in front of us. "Teaching your fairy pet to sit or stay, to not eat your homework, shoes, or dinner, and to come when called are important pet-master skills that you will all be graded on this semester. These skills take time and patience. Why don't we all spend a few moments working with our pets on the sit-and-stay command?"

The classroom gets really loud as people try to keep their pets from trampling them or running out of the classroom. Ollie's parrot is good at flying and landing on command. Peaches refuses to listen.

"Wilson, stay," I tell him, and the mouse looks at me curiously. He's already learned this one. He's so smart. "Good mouse!" I give him another speck of cheese.

A roar from Sasha's tiger cage makes everyone jump, including Headmistress Flora.

"Maybe we will continue this exercise in the courtyard after I introduce our two new students, Jack Spriggins and Allison Grace."

Jack gives a little wave from his chair, but AG actually stands and curtsies.

Behind me, I hear Tessa and Raza giggle.

"Where does the perfect princess think she is? A knight-ing ceremony?" Tessa hisses. "People don't curtsy in class."

AG's smile fades, and she quickly sits down. She clearly heard Tessa. I watch AG's breathing become rapid, and she scratches her arms, which quickly turn red. Look what they're doing to the poor girl! I turn around and glare at Tessa and Raza.

"Leave her alone," I growl, sounding a lot like the puma on the desk across from them. They shut up. I give AG a bright smile. She smiles back, looking relieved.

"New students, the first thing we need you to do is to allow yourself to be picked by a magical fairy pet," says Headmistress Flora. She taps a bookcase on the wall, which flips to reveal a stack of both big and small cages with new pets waiting for owners.

"Come again?" asks Jack, putting his feet up on the desk. Headmistress Flora pushes them off.

"The pet picks you. You don't pick the pet," Jax says in simpler terms.

Jack yawns. "Sounds lame. Besides, I already have a pet—Milky Way, my cow."

"Wasn't your cow taken by Rumpelstiltskin?" someone

asks. At the name, all the animals in the room start to howl and hiss.

Jack stands up. "Yeah. And I'm going to get her back!" He pushes his chair over. "So I don't need another pet! Get it? Butt out!"

I sit back, stunned.

"Mr. Spriggins, that is no way to speak to the class or to me." Flora bristles. "You will allow yourself to be picked by a pet, or you will find yourself in your first detention."

Jack walks to the door. "Then give me detention." His face saddens. "I'm not taking another pet when I already have one I love. I can't do that to her." He slams the door behind him.

Flora looks completely flustered. "Well, I…I must go deal with him, but Allison Grace, why don't you tell the pets about yourself, and one can pick you."

Allison Grace starts to cough. Badly. "Right now? In front of the whole class? But I don't have anything prepared." She pulls at her jumper uncomfortably. The RLWs giggle again.

"Speak from the heart," Flora tells her. Allison Grace looks at her blankly. "Your likes, dislikes, habits. Why don't we—"

"*Mother!*" We hear identical wails as Azalea and Dahlia,

the formerly wicked (depending on who you ask) stepsisters, burst into the classroom like they are apt to do.

"I need a silk tufted pillow to sit on in our Waiting for a Prince to Come class," says Azalea. "How can I sit in a tower all week long when it's made of stone and has no chairs?"

"And I need new oils for my Scents and Sensibility class," says Dahlia. "If I'm going to attract a prince, I need to have the *best* oils to create the *best* perfumes!"

I look at Jax in horror. "Those are actual classes at Royal Academy?"

Jax's smile is grim. "Why do you think I'm so happy not to go to RA anymore?"

"Girls! What have I told you about interrupting me?" Flora ushers them out, but their high-pitched squeals have sent most of the pets into a tizzy. "Gillian, can you please help Allison Grace with her magical fairy pet ceremony? I'll be back soon."

Allison Grace stares mournfully at the cages in front of her.

"Hey," I say with a smile. "Don't worry. You'll get matched with the perfect pet. Look at mine." Wilson peeks out of my pocket. AG reaches out to pet him. "We didn't get along good at first, but now we're a team, just like you'll be with your pet. Let's think about what you can tell these guys to help find your match. It's like Flora says: What do you like, dislike, like to do with friends?"

AG's eyes dart around the room. "I haven't really had many friends up until now. I guess Raz is my friend. She's my godmother."

"Raz as in Rapunzel?" Tessa's mouth gapes.

AG nods. "I've spent some time around her and the other members of the royal court, but I haven't really been anywhere except other castles."

"Woe is me," snorts Raza as her bat flies onto her shoulder. "You're a princess. Your whole life is games and ball gowns." I give her a look to shut her up again.

"Not really." AG stares at her shoes again. "My parents are pretty protective. Up until now, I've been with them all the time."

"Well, your mother let you join a class, so she must be loosening the reins," Jax says. "I grew up in a castle, but I found ways to make it work. What kind of things did you like to do in your ivory tower?"

AG's porcelain face softens. "Like my mother, I read a lot. Not just stories, but travel books too—I've always wanted to see other kingdoms. I'm a decent seamstress, and I like to make accessories out of stuff lying around the castle, like this." She points to the flower in her hair. "I made it from leftover fabric."

"Ooh…" Kayla and Maxine reach for the flower glued to a glittery headband.

"I'm a little tired of the 'I'm a princess, I've been locked away, love me' routine," I hear Tessa say to whoever will listen, including her pet rat. "The princess title has been wasted on that one."

"Are we supposed to bow down to her because she graced us with her presence at FTRS instead of going to RA?" Raza adds. "She's not an actual princess like we follow in the RLWs, so I don't think she should be given special privileges."

"Please let her get a heinous pet," begs Tessa, and a few girls giggle. "Like a snake or a spider or something so not princess perfect!" They all laugh.

I cough loudly so they hear me.

AG touches my arm. "Are you okay?"

"Fine." I side-eye the RLWs watching me. "Back to you, what else can you tell your pet? Do you have any secret talents?"

"Being a wallflower," Tessa whispers, and others giggle. What is with those girls? I hate how jealous they are of AG.

"Well…" AG hesitates, trying to ignore the girls. "When I sing, I can make pumpkins grow." The color in her face deepens.

"Impossible!" Tessa says. "We've been working on that skill in botany all year, and none of us have mastered it." Girls around her nod. "My voice is the most beautiful in the school, and I can't do it."

"Beautiful if you're listening underwater," Jocelyn mumbles.

"I've done it before." AG sounds suddenly unsure. "Maybe it was beginner's luck."

Everyone is talking over each other now, and Ollie runs outside and grabs a pumpkin from our vegetable patch. "Here!" He sets the small green-and-orange pumpkin on the desk in front of her. "Try it on this one."

AG backs away. "I don't know."

Anna used to be shy like this. Maybe if I had helped her become more confident, she wouldn't have been so unsure of herself all the time. We have to toughen this girl up if she's going to survive here. "You can do it!" I say. "Try it!"

AG takes a deep breath. "My pumpkins always liked the song 'My Prince Will Wait for Me.'"

"Is she kidding me?" Raza whispers.

"Please let her get a snake!" Tessa says again.

AG starts singing. Her voice is buttery and light, like a fine violin. Even the pets grow quiet. The little pumpkin starts to grow larger and larger until it gets so big that it threatens to break the desk.

When she's done, we all cheer. AG curtsies. Tessa's and Raza's mouths are hanging open. A fly zooms into Raza's mouth, and she starts to cough. Soon the cages in front of us begin to glow and glitter. We wait and watch with interest to see what comes out, but nothing appears out of the darkness.

"Look at that. None of the pets wanted her," Raza says, and she and Tessa giggle.

Suddenly the back door bursts open and a white unicorn with a purple mane comes galloping into the classroom, coming to a halt in front of AG. It neighs softly, its golden horn brushing against her cheek.

"Wow, aren't you beautiful! Hello!" AG pets the unicorn gently. "We have to give you a name, don't we?"

"No one has gotten a unicorn before!" Kayla marvels, as most of our classmates gather around to see the mystical creature. "It's the perfect pet for a princess!"

"Nice job," I tell AG, giving her a hug. I knew she could do it.

Everyone is gathered around AG, patting her on the back and marveling at her unicorn. Everyone, that is, except Tessa and Raza.

Happily Ever After Scrolls

Brought to you by Fairy Web—Enchantasia's

Number One News Source!

Meet the beauty who tamed the beast—FTRS's new librarian!

by Coco Collette

Name: Beauty, or B to her close friends and family, is the book-loving maiden who stole Prince Sebastian's heart and broke his nightmarish curse!

Occupation: Helping her husband run a kingdom is a full-time job, as is being a mother to eleven-year-old daughter, Allison Grace. It was during her years spent homeschooling Allison Grace that she realized she had a talent she could use to help others. "I don't just love books. I need them the way some people need air," Beauty says with a laugh. "I want to pass that love on to others and share my knowledge of our private library with lots of children. When Princess Ella approached me about running Fairy Tale Reform School's new library, I knew it was the perfect place for me and our family."

Hobbies: Like her husband, travel is high on her list ("I love any chance to explore someplace new.") and books of course! FTRS's library, which Beauty curated from her own private collection, has some rather unique tomes. Rumor has it books come alive! Beauty was mum on the subject, saying only, "I've always believed books were magical."

Strengths: Beauty prides herself on being a great listener. She also knows how to calm the moody Prince Sebastian and the secret to helping tame his beastly side. "We recently both took up yoga, and it's helped us a lot."

Weaknesses: "I hate when someone is small-minded," she says, blushing. "People should always be open to new perspectives and experiences."

Check back soon for more coverage on Fairy Tale Reform School!

CHAPTER 6

Lost in the Library

Ꙩ

My boots echo on the cobblestone floors as I trudge to the library. I hear a loud cheer coming from the FTRS fields where a rugby match is going on. Pretty much the whole school is there, so I'll have the library to myself, which is just what I want. It's time I find a book on You-Know-Who and figure out what he might be planning.

I walk quickly past two elves hanging precariously off a floating ladder. They're trying to get a mirror hung on the wall. It begins to glow bright purple as they try to center it.

"Gilly? Oh good, there you are!" Miri says.

I stop short. Does she somehow know what I'm up to? Can she hear thoughts now too?

"Just off to the library to work on a paper for Prince Sebastian," I cheerfully fudge.

"You have ignored two notices to bring your spare uniform to the seamstress to be updated with the new school crest. One more reminder, and I'll have to sentence you to detention." She tsks. "Shall I put you down for tomorrow at ten a.m.?" Miri asks brightly. "Since you'll be at school this weekend while your friends are allowed to leave?"

I ball up my fists. After one week of classes, Prince Sebastian decided Jax, Maxine, and Ollie were the first three students worthy of getting to go home for the weekend. Their weekend pass scrolls came this morning, glowing bright with the words:

Great job! Enjoy a weekend at home!
6:00 p.m. pickup!

Kayla and Jocelyn are still here, but I doubt I'll see Jocelyn. ("Not having to deal with all of you for a weekend is vacation enough for me," she said.) "I guess so," I tell Miri.

"Great! Don't forget!"

Her mirror goes as dark as my mood. I stomp to the library double doors and give them a tug, but they won't budge. I pull harder and still nothing. I give them one more yank, and *boom*! The doors fly open with Prince Sebastian and AG behind them.

"Hi, Gilly!" AG says. I freeze. "I was just telling Father how you gave me my nickname! And how you helped me pick out my unicorn. I named her Butterscotch because it's my favorite ice cream flavor. Isn't that a lovely name?"

Prince Sebastian eyes me suspiciously.

I manage a smile. "Beautiful! But you're the one who showed Butterscotch your true colors. That's why she picked you. It had nothing to do with me."

"I still think you helped," AG insists. "We're heading out to watch the rugby game. We're sitting in Raz's royal seats. She's here representing Royal Academy, but I think she really wants to root for FTRS, don't you? Want to join us?"

AG sounds so much happier and open than she did a day ago. I'm so glad, but the thought of sitting in the RA box is too much for me to bear. I may be friendly with royals now, but I'm still not interested in watching a rugby match from the snooty royal school's seats with the royal court watching my every move. There's too good a chance I'll screw up. "I actually need to stay at the library to work on my family tree paper." I don't make eye contact with the prince.

"The library closes at nine, you know," Prince Sebastian says, insinuating I need way more time than I have to do a paper that will impress him.

"That gives me three hours. Considering I don't have privileges to go home this weekend, I have plenty of time to work on my project," I say innocently.

I could swear the prince growls.

"You're staying here for the weekend? Are you around tomorrow?" AG asks hopefully. "Mother said I could have a friend over to the castle."

"You didn't ask me if you could have anyone over," Prince Sebastian points out.

"*Father*." AG looks down at the glittery, silver shoes on her feet. "Mother said it was fine."

"It is fine, but I want to know who you're hanging out with in this new kingdom."

"It's just Gilly, Father." AG rolls her eyes at me like I'm in on the joke.

I see the look the prince is giving me and can tell he doesn't approve of me as AG's new friend. I wish he'd give me a shot. I genuinely like AG and am just trying to help her fit in. Maybe if I had done that with Anna in the village, she wouldn't have fallen in with those candy thieves Hansel and Gretel.

"We shall see," the prince says. "Allison Grace, I forgot my wand in my office. I want it for the game in case any danger arises."

"At a rugby match?" I ask.

He ignores me. "Shall I meet you in Raz's box?" he asks AG.

"Yes, Father," AG says. "I'll meet you there." With a nod to me and a kiss on AG's cheek, he walks away just as the library doors creak open again.

"Allison Grace?" It's Beauty. She's carrying a large stack of books that teeter precariously. "Could you help me with these… Oh! A visitor."

"Hello," I say anxiously, wondering if Beauty will remember me from our ill-fated first meeting.

"Would you mind helping me and Allison Grace put these books away?" Beauty's smile is so bright and welcoming. How can I say no?

"Sure." I take several books off the top of the stack and

study the title on top: *While You Were Sleeping: What Really Happens during a Sleeping Curse.*

"Thank you! You're Gilly, aren't you?" Beauty says, and I wait for her expression to change to disapproval. Instead, her smile widens. "AG told us how you gave her a nickname and helped with her unicorn." She puts a warm hand on my shoulder. "Raz tells us AG couldn't have picked better in the friend department." Beauty disappears into a stack to restock books.

A fairy with flaxen hair that smells like fresh linens flutters to my side. "What may I help you find today?"

"Brooke Lynn, this is Gilly," AG explains. "She's helping Mother and me in the stacks."

"Oh, hi!" the fairy says. "You're Kayla's friend, right?"

"And you're one of Kayla's sisters."

The fairy nods. She looks a few years older than Kayla. "We can't thank you enough for all you did to help break our curse," Brooke Lynn gushes. Beauty steps out of the stacks to listen. "Mother has been dying to have you to our fairy hut for dinner."

I try hard not to blush. Kayla made me promise not to tell anyone what happened with her mother the other night. Her mother hasn't mentioned seeing me or that book she was talking about again, so Kayla thinks she's forgotten the whole thing. As far as Kayla's family knows, I've never been to their fairy hut.

"A fairy hut?" AG's eyes widen. "I've always wanted to see one of those."

"I'm just glad Kayla has her family back." The word *family* catches in my throat, and I quickly clear it so no one gets the wrong idea that I was about to cry or anything. Beauty watches me curiously. "Maybe AG and I could both come visit this weekend."

"Of course," Brooke Lynn says warmly. "Kayla would love it." She eyes my now-empty hands.

"So what book can I help you find?"

Everyone looks at me. Now is not the time to say I need a book on You-Know-Who.

"I'm not sure," I lie. "I am working on my family tree project, so I have to poke around."

Brooke Lynn nods. "First floor only. Upper floors have to be approved by teachers or the librarian." She smiles at Beauty. "Let me know if you need help." I hear a bell tinkling somewhere in the library, and she flutters off to help someone else.

"Are you working on your family tree project?" AG asks. "Mother and I have been working on mine, but I am happy to help you with yours. Did you bring what you have so far?" She spies the bag on my back.

The thought of anyone seeing my empty tree is more than I can bear. I place my hand on my bag protectively. "I still have a lot of work to do." Beauty is still looking at me. "But I'll show you when I'm done."

"Okay." AG sounds shy again. "I should probably meet Father at the game anyway." She kisses her mother on the cheek, and her mother hugs her. I feel a pang of longing at the simple gesture, one I could have had this weekend if the Beast hadn't decided otherwise. "See you later, Gilly!" She bounds off, a spring in her step that I envy.

"She's really nice," I say, and I mean it.

"She's had a rough time making friends in the past." Beauty's pale brow suddenly furrows. "She can be a bit shy, but when you get to know her, she has a great sense of humor, just like her father." I must make a face because Beauty laughs.

"I guess you haven't seen his humorous side yet," she says. "Sebastian can be a bit stubborn, but once he sees in you what

AG does, I think you'll find he can be an excellent teacher. He's quite smart." She looked around the large library. "I wouldn't be surprised if he's read biographies on every hero and villain there is in here."

Villain. Stiltskin. "Have you read all their biographies too?" I ask now that we're alone.

"Not as many as Sebastian." Beauty's eyes are big and curious. "All these books came from our private library, so I'm always finding something new to read, whether it's a text-book or a fairy tale. Villain stories don't interest me as much."

This is my in. I have to play my cards carefully though. "Really? I thought all princesses like to know the villains they're up against."

"Well, I wasn't a princess until I married Sebastian," Beauty says thoughtfully. "So I'm a bit different."

Gingerbread. I knew that. Let me try again. "I think I'd like reading about villains." Beauty looks at me. "Since I've had to fight a few here already, it helps to know what makes them tick, you know?"

Beauty frowns. "I've learned to not always trust what you read about villains. Now heroes, on the other hand, I have a lot of material on." Beauty hurries ahead, jumping on a moving ladder and plucking a gold, yellow, and red book off the top shelf. "How about a book about Aladdin? Or Hua Mulan?"

I put my hand on a rotating bannister as Brooke Lynn passes me with a new stack of books. On an upper floor I see her sister, Emma Rose, and their mother working at a library station. I'm not going to get past them on my own, not with Beauty keeping watch. Should I just be honest? Can I trust her? Here goes nothing. "I bet those are great, but the person that would make the most sense for me to read about would be Rumpelstiltskin."

Brooke Lynn drops the stack of books she's carrying. Beauty's smile wavers.

"I have good reason to include information on him on my family tree," I blurt out. "My sister left FTRS a few months ago to join his Stiltskin Squad, and I can't understand why. Why would anyone want to trust a goblin or troll like him? If I could just read more about him and see what his allure is, maybe I could figure it out." I don't mean to sound so desperate, but I am.

Beauty smiles sadly. "I am sorry to hear about your sister, but unfortunately, you can't take villain books out without teacher permission. Have you asked Headmistress Flora if you can read a book on Rumpelstiltskin?" Brooke Lynn gives another audible gasp. "Sorry! Maybe we should call him something else."

"Tricky, family-stealing troll?" I suggest, and Beauty smirks. "I just want to know where he comes from, how long he's been in the kingdom, what he could be planning that my sister will be a part of."

"Don't worry! The royal court is on top of all that," Beauty says. "That was part of the appeal for us coming here. Sebastian has long hoped to track the angry, family-stealing troll too."

"Really?" I say, surprised.

Beauty sits down, a stack of books in her lap. "Not many people know Rumpelstiltskin was the one who cursed the prince when he was young. He was a different man back then. Selfish. Arrogant. Only concerned for himself and his own needs. Stiltskin used that to his advantage, and long story short, Sebastian was cursed to live his life as a beast."

"I didn't know that." What else do I not know about the prince? "So you see why I want to read about Stiltskin. It's just a book I'm after."

"Nothing is ever just a book," Beauty says lightly. "Books

transport us to other places. They make us believe anything is possible. Villain origin stories can sometimes make us believe the darkest things are also possible. While nothing is out of the question, Flora asked that only the highest level of students—those who can't be swayed by anything a villain tells them—be allowed access to those books." She gives me a sympathetic smile. "I'm sorry, but I don't believe your name is on that list."

"How do I get it on that list?" I try again.

"Gillian," Beauty says patiently. "I don't mean to overstep, but I know about your sister and how hard the royal court is trying to find Rumpelstiltskin and his squad. Finding some-one takes time, I'm afraid, especially if that someone does not want to be found."

"Do you mean my sister or him?" I ask quietly.

"Perhaps both," says Beauty. "You are an important part of this school's story, so you are bound to this place, but you have to understand your sister may be on a different path from your own."

"But we're sisters," I say. "She has to be wired for good. I am."

"I hope you're right," Beauty says. "Why don't you tell

me more about her? Did you bring what you have done for the project so far?" She motions to a desk floating a few feet off the ground. She floats a chair over to me so I can sit next to her.

"I'm not ready to show it to anyone yet." *Because I don't have anything done.*

"I am not here to judge. I'm a great listener." Beauty pats the chair next to her. "Maybe we can find some books to help you finish it without having to read a book on Rumpelstiltskin."

It's hard to say no to a professor who is also a princess. I unroll my parchment.

I'm embarrassed, but I show her the empty tree with Mother's and Father's names at the roots. That's all I've really done. Per the prince's instructions, my brothers' and sisters' names, along with mine, should be filled in. There should also be Father's likes and dislikes, information on the shop, and what Mother cooks for dinner. Since this is supposed to be more than a chart, I should also include smells, like what our boot's scent is (shoe leather, of course). I should include information on my grandfather and grandmother and how they had a shoe business and how my grandmother went to a fairy godmother training school, but I haven't done any of that yet. I can't get myself to sit down and do it.

Beauty thumbs the bare tree. "You don't have anything to say about your family?"

I was planning to keep quiet, but the words come out in a great big rush. "No, because I'm angry with my family! For Father not finding Anna! For Mother being foolish enough to believe Anna is fine because she got a Pegasus Post saying so! For my brothers and sisters not understanding what is going on! And I'm mad at Anna for choosing him over her family!" Wow, it felt good to say all that out loud.

"You have every right to be mad, but what you're talking about is the present. This project is about your past." Beauty places a finger on the spot where my FTRS schooling should go, along with any honors I've received. "You weren't always mad at them. What was your relationship like with Anna before?"

I push the scroll away. "I don't remember."

"Don't or won't?" she asks. I don't answer. "The past can be a tricky place to revisit, especially when it hurts. Why don't you tell me about your other siblings. Who is Hamish?"

I can't help but smile. "He tells the best jokes, but Felix

is the one who knows how to fix anything, and Trixie has the best voice you've ever heard—well, other than AG's. And Anna—" I catch myself. Beauty almost tricked me. "I don't want to talk about her."

I see a fairy shutting down her station for the night. Aren't they open till nine?

"Regardless of what happened, she's still your sister," Beauty says. "You must have enjoyed doing things with her."

"Maybe." I turn my eyes away from the empty tree trunk on the scroll. "But it was all a lie."

"Why do you say that?"

I'd rather hide in a stack than talk about this, but Beauty's face is so kind that I find myself opening up. "Because for the longest time, I thought she was happy, and it turns out she wasn't. I thought all she cared about was her Rapunzel idolization and her cute hair clips and being with her friends. But she secretly felt like she was living in my shadow and I was taking her chance at running Father's shop away from her.

"I want nothing to do with shoes or the shop. I want Anna to have it, but now she's not even here to tell all of this to! She's gone, and I'm not sure she's ever coming back, so there's no chance I'll be interviewing her for this project, which means I'm going to fail and get kicked out of the MMC program." I feel the tears spring to my eyes. "But do you know what the worst part is? Now I can't tell her how sorry I am that I made her feel that way. If she knew that, she'd come back. I know she would." I feel hot tears run down my face.

Beauty pulls me into a hug. At first, I resist, but then I slowly fall into the curves of her shoulders, letting my face get smashed by her long, sweet-smelling locks. I cry as she strokes my hair like Mother would if I were home. I didn't realize how badly I needed a hug till just this moment.

"Sometimes a good cry makes everything feel better," Beauty says.

"I'm not a crier." I wipe my eyes with the back of my sleeve.

"But it felt good, right?" she asks.

"Yes," I admit. I stare at my parchment, which now has tearstains on it. "I keep thinking about how good Anna would do in the prince's class. She's always known what she wanted to be. But me, I still have no clue."

"But you know who you *don't* want to be—a villain, a thief, a pickpocket." Beauty points to the me section of my family tree—the only part I've filled in about myself—where

I've listed my previous, um, achievements. "And you know what you're good at." She motions to where I've listed archery, fencing, and adventure as well as my favorite class at FTRS, history. "If you keep exploring, I think you'll find what you're looking for. Don't rush it," she says. "That's what I've been telling Allison Grace. You're lucky to get to try so many classes and ideas on for size. The right path for you will show itself eventually."

I spontaneously hug her. It's a move out of character for me, but it feels natural with Beauty. "Thank you for listening and for trying to help."

"Of course. I just want you to know you're not alone," Beauty says. "My door is always open. The library is open nine a.m. to nine p.m., but you can visit our pop-up castle anytime." A light goes off behind us, and she laughs. "With the rugby game, you're our first visitor in hours, so we're going to close the library early."

I guess tonight is not the night I'll find a way to beat Rumpelstiltskin, but I still learned something important— Beauty might be the wisest royal of them all.

Gilly,

Tried to swim into the Fairy Tale Reform School lake to get a message to you faster, but the entrance is magically blocked. I had to resort to these Pegasus Posts. I had to pay to send you one! Fishy, if you ask me.

After I returned from FTRS, we took a family swim trip to the North Star Sea. Stiltskin was there on a ship with a whole crew of kids! I was scared he'd spot me, so I hid behind rocks. I watched them cast nets for hours. They came back day after day. They were looking for something, but their nets kept coming up empty.

One night, I swam up to their boat to try to get some intel. I peeked through a porthole and saw Stiltskin in there with his crew. He angrily ripped a map to pieces, saying everyone wasn't searching hard enough for some book. The kids claimed they'd searched land and sea, but couldn't find the book or the music that he sought. (Music under the sea? Everyone knows you can't hear a mermaid sing unless you have Shell Service.) Stiltskin finally said it was time to "go back to base." Then he threw what looked like beans on the floor. They looked like the ones we found in his office!

I'm not sure what he's up to, Gilly, but be careful. Whatever he has planned for Enchantasia, it isn't over yet.

—Hayley

CHAPTER 7

You Don't Know Jack

ook what I got!" Jocelyn waves a scroll in the air as she
approaches our table in the cafeteria. I can see the spar-
kling A from here. "Top marks from Prince Sebastian on my
'Mirror, Mirror' assignment. What did you get, Gilly?" She
sits down and stares at me with glee.

She knows what I got. A big, fat F that glows like a bright-
red, flaming letter! It's impossible to hide the grade when it
shoots flames. I hold up the scroll since Jocelyn is waiting
expectantly, and Jax, Ollie, and Kayla lean over Maxine to see it.

Around us, elves are clearing plates, spraying down messy
tables with ELF cleaning spray, and trying to usher us out the
door so the wood sprites can do the rest of the cleanup before
dinner. In the kitchen, I can hear the cooks washing dishes. A

large pot from a kitchen supply closet behind me floats over my head and into the kitchen area.

"What does it say in that tiny print?" Jocelyn asks innocently. "I can't read it. Mine says 'Great sense of self at such a young age. Continue to dig deep! Well done!'"

I sigh and begin to read the flaming note: "'Failure to follow instructions and resistance to accept oneself leads to poor marks. Try harder.'"

Jocelyn laughs wickedly.

"Jocelyn, stop being so mean," Maxine tells her, a piece of spinach from the salad she had at lunch still caught between her teeth. She eyes the half of a brownie on Jocelyn's plate. "Are you going to eat that?" Jocelyn forks it over before an elf takes her plate.

"It's not fair," I complain. "This whole class was my idea, and the prince is out to get me. I don't deserve an F, do I?"

Jax reads over my scroll again and grimaces. "You only wrote two sentences, and one was 'I have no clue what you want me to write.' Why would he give you a better grade when you didn't do any work?"

"Whose side are you on?" I grumble. "I've had a lot on my mind, okay? First, I got that Pegasus Post from Mother and then one from Hayley this morning." I quickly fill them in.

"What would he be looking for in the North Star Sea?" Kayla asks as she spears a forkful of lettuce. "He already has beans."

"Aye," Ollie says. "But the sea holds many treasures. Who knows what someone might have buried under the ocean. What's this book he's talking about?"

"I don't know," I admit. "If it's a book he's after, you'd think it'd be in our new library. There are thousands. Not that I can get my hands on the ones I want."

"No one is going to hand you a Stiltskin book," Jocelyn reminds me. "You have to be stealthy if you want one of those."

Quack!

Peaches picks her head up from under the table like she's an alarm.

Quack! Quack!

Jack is wandering around the cafeteria, his lunch tray hovering alongside him as he looks for a seat. No one is waving him over. A troll spreads out across the bench he's on so there is no room for anyone else to sit. I decide to take pity on him.

"Jack! Come sit with us." I wave.

Jax groans.

"What? He seems nice."

"Nice?" Jax scoffs as he peels an apple with a paring knife with one smooth move. "He's already had detention three times for talking back to teachers, and he walked out of Magical Fairy Pets because he refused to be paired up with an animal. I don't like the guy."

"He's having a hard time adjusting," I whisper as Jack sits and his tray floats down in front of him. "I did too. Be nice. Jack, these are my friends Jocelyn, Maxine, Ollie, Kayla, and Jax." Everyone says hello or waves.

Jack's napkin magically ties around his neck as Peaches begins nudging the bag that he's placed at his feet. "Leave that alone, you ugly duckling!"

"Peaches is not ugly," Maxine says with a huff. "She's unique."

Jack eyes the duck suspiciously, then shrugs. "Your duck. Think what you want."

"So Jax—I mean Jack—how are you settling in?" Kayla asks politely. "Sorry. Your names are so similar."

"They are!" Ollie agrees. "Jax and Jack. Jack and Jax. Jack-Jax!"

"Our names are not similar at all." Jack eyes his new nemesis. "I've never even heard of a Jax before. It's so stuffy."

Jocelyn laughs.

"It's Jaxon," Jax says curtly. "*Prince* Jaxon."

"Oh, excuse me, Your Excellency." Jack stands up and bows.

Peaches takes that moment to dig into Jack's bag. I don't say anything. I'm too worried about these two brawling.

"So, Jack, how long are you in for?" I ask.

"I'm hoping the shortest stay possible," he says. "I have to get out of here and go find my mum. I don't want her around Rumpelstiltskin for too long, you know?"

"I spent years searching for my family after he took them," Kayla says, her face darkening. "He's a hard man to pin down."

"The royal court will find him," Jax says. "We just have to be patient."

"Thank you for your words of wisdom, *Prince*," Jack says, "but her sister is missing. My mom and cow have been taken. Why should we wait around for the royals to find answers when we can find them ourselves?"

Maxine claps excitedly. "Ooh! An adventure! Are you saying we should go look for Stiltskin?"

"No!" Jax sounds exasperated. "Last time we barely survived giants and a bandersnatch."

"You're scared of a giant?" Jack laughs out loud. "I've already defeated one of those monsters."

"So you claim." Jax glares at him, and Jack glares back. "And besides, it's not just giants out there. We'd have to go up against Stiltskin head on, and we've never done that before. I don't think we'd get away so easily."

"Magic carpet racing starts in ten minutes!" Blackbeard bellows from the open doorway. "All ye lads and lasses who want in, better be swift! Aye, only taking first ten on each line." There's a huge rush for the door. Our table is the only one that stays seated.

"Since when are you afraid of a challenge?" I ask, feeling prickly.

"I just don't think we should go looking for trouble without a reason," Jax says. "Until we find Anna and the others, or learn what book Stiltskin is looking for, there's no point going on a Mother Goose chase. Other than Hayley's sighting, there's been no sign of Stiltskin since he left FTRS, which means he's cooking up something more awful than we can imagine."

"I heard he was after some magic beans," says Jack, and

my ears perk up. He didn't hear Hayley's Pegasus Post. If he knows about the beans, maybe he has more intel to share. "Maybe he's planning on growing a beanstalk."

Jax ignores him and looks at me. "I think my sister is right. We have to know what he's after before we put a move into play."

"You think the royal court cares about Stiltskin if he's not a threat at this exact moment?" Jack asks, chomping on his turkey leg. "You think they care about my mum or cow?"

"Or Anna?" I ask quietly.

"They care about all their subjects," Jax says.

Jocelyn and I groan. "I hate when you use that word," I grumble. "Like we're slaves!"

Jack and Jocelyn burst out laughing, and Jax looks like he's going to explode.

"I'm sorry, but there's more at stake here than just your sister," Jax snaps, and I inhale sharply. "I don't mean to be hurtful, but it's true. Miri is hunting every mirror in the land to find out what that troll is up to. We have to stay put and let everyone gather the intel. He's too tricky to out-trick twice."

"But what if Anna changed her mind and wants to come

back but can't? I can't just leave her out there till the royal court is ready to make a move."

"You have to learn to trust other people sometimes," Jax says, sounding a lot like the governing princesses.

I fold my arms. "I guess this is the first time we don't agree on something."

"I guess so," Jax says evenly.

Quack! We turn around and see Peaches pulling something small and shiny out of Jack's bag. It's the gold mirror he had the other day.

"Hey!" he shouts as Peaches swallows it whole. "My mirror!"

Peaches gives a large burp.

"Give it back," Jack shouts, lunging for the duck.

Maxine jumps up from the table and stands in Jack's path. She's twice the size of him. "Leave my duck alone."

"Your duck ate my mirror!" Jack says, lunging again for Peaches, who tries to bite his fingers. "I need it back! Make her cough it up."

"She never coughs up items," Maxine lies, and Peaches hides behind her. "At least not in one piece. If you want me to send you the parts once she's done with them, I can do that."

"Eww, no, forget it." Jack looks like he has some ideas on how he'd get the mirror out of Peaches. "I'm going out to watch the magic carpet races." He starts to walk away.

"Duck!" I shout, which may be a poor choice of word.

The rest of us crouch as a dozen soup spoons fly across the room to the kitchen. Jack gets hit in the back with a spoon, and Jax actually laughs. I shoot him a nasty look and walk over to Jack to check on him.

"Come on. I'll help you outside," I say, leaving my friends at the table.

On the great lawn behind the cafeteria, kids are already getting their aggression out. A group of kids are playing Fight the Knight with a bewitched scarecrow dressed up for a sword fight. (Every time a kid gets close to nailing it with a sword, the scarecrow bobs and weaves.) RLWs are singing to the pumpkin patch to try to make the pumpkins grow like AG did. Blackbeard is setting up a pirate challenge near the lake, where kids can slide off the plank and hold themselves up by their arms over the water. (It works the core muscles or something like that.) And near the fields, I see elves setting up the magic carpet racing track.

Neither Jack nor I seem in the mood to rush over

and play, so we find a spot on the grass by the vegetable garden.

"Sorry if I was rough with your friends back there," Jack says. "I don't mean to be. I'm just so worried about my mum and Milky Way. I can't think of anything but finding them. No one cares about getting that troll as much as I do."

"*I do*," I say, and Jack looks at me. "Ever since my sister decided to leave school with Rumpelstiltskin, I can't stop thinking about how I could have convinced her to stay here."

He looks at me. "Then you know why I need to get out of this place and find him." I nod. "We can't wait for the stuffy royal court to do something!" He looks at his beat-up boots. "Look, I have a confession to make: I got thrown into FTRS on purpose." I stare at him in surprise. "I thought he was still in control of this place, and my mum might be here. Instead, he's gone and the only villain in this joint is some stone statue I've never seen."

"Alva," I explain. "The wicked fairy. She was turned to stone during a battle we had at school. She guards the dungeon, so to speak. I thought I saw her statue move once, but I think I was just seeing things."

"The dungeon," Jack repeats. "I guess that's the best place to keep a villain. Even one encased in stone. I wonder if the Stiltskin Squad has learned how to turn people to stone yet." He frowns. "I hope they don't try it with my mum."

"You know about the Stiltskin Squad too?" I ask.

"Doesn't everybody?" Jack plucks a daisy and rips off its flowers. "It's his army. They do whatever he asks of them."

This is hard to admit, but Jack might be the only other person at this school who can understand what I'm going through. "My sister is a member," I say quietly.

He runs a hand through his short black hair. "I know."

I sit straight up. My heart starts to beat faster. "How do you know that?"

"Anna Cobbler, right?" Jack asks. "I saw her with him. Back when he stole my mum and Milky Way. He called her by name. She's the one"—his voice chokes up—"that hand-cuffed my mum."

My stomach begins to hurt. "She's not evil," I insist. "She's just confused! He promised her so much, and she believes him. At least, she did before. I haven't spoken to her, so I have no idea how she feels now."

"We have to find them," says Jack, his breathing growing shallow. "Rescue them, talk sense into them. Do whatever it takes to get them away from Rumpelstiltskin. What are we waiting for?" He stands up quickly, and I grab his wrist.

Something is holding me back. It's like I can hear Jax's voice in my head. *It's a wild-goose chase.* "As much as I hate to admit it, Jax is right. We need more information before we bust out of here and try to find them. We have no clue where to look."

Jack sits back down. He grabs my hands and holds them tight. "Gilly, there is something I should mention about your sister…"

I squeeze his hands. "Tell me."

"She might have gone with him willingly, but I don't think she wants to stay in the squad anymore," Jack whispers.

"How do you know that?" I ask, scared to hear the answer.

"Anna was the only one who fought back when Stiltskin wanted my mum," Jack tells me. "She tried to stop him. It made me think she didn't agree with his ways."

That's the sister I remember, I think with pride. "Did he hurt her?" I ask.

Jack shakes his head. "No, but he was mad. He said she'd pay for disagreeing with him."

My stomach begins to twist and turn. I can feel the anger bubbling up inside me.

His brown eyes look at me sadly. "Don't you see? It's time we get them all out of there before it's too late."

CHAPTER 8

The Newest RLW

So then I said to myself, 'What would a princess do?' And I knew immediately if I called to the songbirds, they'd fly to my tower window and bring me the pink scarf I dropped. And they did!"

This is the story Raza is telling a group of rapt RLWs when Maxine and I walk into the meeting. A dozen girls in pink sashes are sitting on the floor listening as she tells her tale from the fluffy, pink armchair reserved for our club adviser, Rapunzel. The girls—and Ollie—are hanging on her every word.

"I actually saw the scarf fall," Ollie brags, his RLW sash flashing the word *lad* in bright-yellow letters.

"See?" Raza says brightly, giving Tessa a sharp look. "My story is true."

"So I grabbed a magic carpet and raced up to deliver it," Ollie adds.

"*No*," Raza says sharply. "A *songbird* brought it up. We have a connection since my magical fairy pet is a flier as well."

"Your fairy pet is a bat," Tessa points out, and a few girls gasp.

"It has wings," Raza sneers. "Same difference." She looks at Ollie. "And the bird brought it to me. Not you." Ollie opens his mouth to protest. "*Anyway*," Raza says loudly, "I clearly have princess talents since a songbird flew to my vicinity when I was in need."

I roll my eyes. "Why do I have to stay in this club again?"

Maxine puts a meaty arm around me. "So we can hang out together more."

"We're already roommates."

"But this is the only club I'm in with you! You know I can't do fencing with these hands." She motions to her large fingers. "I can barely grasp the sword. And you'd be pretty bad at Castle Storming. It requires major upper-body strength."

I nod. The last thing on my mind right now is clubs. All I can think about is what Jack said about Anna. She's good! I knew she was! And she wants to get away from

Rumpelstiltskin. Now that I know that, I have to get to her. I'm dying to tell Maxine what Jack said, but I'm not sure she'll believe him. I know Jax wouldn't.

"What's wrong?" Maxine asks, her brow crinkling. "Are you thinking about Rumpelstiltskin again?" I hear a chorus of gasps.

"Maxine?" Tessa marches up to us, her uniform skirt unusually swishy and large, and whispers so that only we can hear. "Could you please not mention the former headmaster who tried to corrupt our entire school in the RLWs' presence? You know how much it upsets us."

I roll my eyes. "That's ridiculous! We can't pretend it didn't happen! We lost two RLWs to that evil troll." I stand up and stare at the others. "Finding that trickster is way more important than picking out towels for the bathrooms. Students are just going to steal them anyway!" There are more gasps and Tessa narrows her eyes at me, but I don't care. Jack stirred something inside me that I can't deny anymore. I might be the only one who can help my sister.

Maxine tries to steer me away from the line of fire. "You're cranky, and when I'm cranky, a snack always helps." She offers me a plate of pink cookies, but I shake my head.

Ollie walks over and pours me a glass of pink lemonade. That I take, gulping it loudly.

"Feel better?" Raza asks, surveying me unkindly. "Good. Now I understand you miss your sister. We miss the RLWs we lost too, but crying over them into a cloth napkin is so uncivilized!" She whips out an embroidered handkerchief. "If we must cry, it should be into one of these, which the club lovingly embroidered at our last meeting. The RLWs have spent a great deal of time hand-stitching handkerchiefs with the letters *FTRS*, and I think it's done a lot to lift everyone's mood. Just because we go to a reform school is no reason for our bathrooms to be anything but beautiful."

The other members agree.

"We should all do our parts to make sure they aren't stolen." Raza looks directly at me with her beady goblin eyes.

"Raza? Can I just say, I love the fresh flowers we've added to the bathrooms," Maxine gushes.

"Me too," adds Ollie. "The flowers mask the fart smell in the boys' bathrooms."

Raza ignores his remark. "Tessa has been putting fresh flowers in the bathrooms for weeks. Millie and Maxine have been adding baskets of fresh potpourri. Ollie is tackling the boys' rooms. Maxine even donated some jewelry for girls to liven up their bland school uniforms." She crosses her arms and looks at me. "What have *you* been doing, Gilly?"

"Helping me," a sweet voice says.

AG is standing in the doorway. She curtsies, and everyone rises fast to curtsy to the actual princess in our midst.

"Gilly's been so busy helping me to settle in and understand my coursework that she hasn't had much time for bathroom duty," says AG, a small smile playing on her lips.

She's making a joke! And I'm in on it. This AG might not be as shy as I think.

"Exactly," I say solemnly. "I've become the princess's unofficial school tour guide."

"Is this the Royal Ladies-in-Waiting meeting?" AG asks, looking at the pink wallpaper, pink chandelier, and pink chairs, tablecloths, and curtains. "Or do you all just like to hang out in a very pink room?"

"Yes," says Tessa. She looks at Raza so quickly I could blink and miss it. "But it's a club for members who aspire to help royals, not actual royals. I don't think you would like it much, being a royal and all."

"Really? Raz invited me." AG walks in farther. "Wow, there really is a lot of pink in here. Who decorated this room?"

"Me," Tessa says fiercely. "It follows the RLW code. Pink is a princess's favorite color."

"Not all princesses," AG points out. "I prefer blue."

I am loving this.

Raza stammers. "Well, it's a favorite of the princesses that *we* serve. Maybe your kingdom is different."

"AG, you made it!" Rapunzel sweeps into the room in a lilac dress, carrying a basket of teacups. She gives her goddaughter a kiss on the cheek. Tessa looks like her head might explode. "Everyone, I take it you've met AG. She's going to be joining the RLWs."

Raza clears her throat. "Rapunzel? I thought the club was just for those who wanted to serve the royals. Can a royal serve herself?" Many RLWs nod.

"We let boys in this year, didn't we?" Rapunzel replies, and Ollie waves to the room as a reminder. "I see no reason why royals can't join us if their goal is to help change the kingdom. And AG knows what it means to make a change more than most of us."

"No, I don't!" AG blurts out. Her voice is frightened. "I haven't changed one bit! Have I?"

Rapunzel touches AG's hand. "I meant change as in moving, dear. You made a huge change when your family moved to a new kingdom, no?"

AG smiles with relief. "Right. Of course. I knew what you meant." She looks down at her hands.

How strange. I glance at Maxine, who is busy trying to swat a fly away with her hand.

"But back to today's task: we will focus on tea service." Rapunzel gestures for us to take a seat at the long, pink table. She takes teacups out of her basket and places one in front of each girl. "How does one serve tea? Properly pour tea? And how does an RLW create the perfect garden party?"

Millie gasps. "Tell me we're having a tea party! Tell me we're having *any* kind of party."

Collectively, the RLWs look at Rapunzel, who grins. "Yes. We are having a tea party!" The girls squeal. "One to welcome our newest Fairy Tale Reform School family, Prince Sebastian, Princess Beauty, and their daughter, our very own AG, who is now an official member of the RLWs!"

Rapunzel places an RLW sash over AG's head. We

applaud as AG blushes. All of us but Tessa and Raza. Tessa's green-hued skin actually turns greener when Rapunzel asks AG to sit next to her. Suddenly, the pair of them are up and trying to get people to switch seats so they can be by AG.

"I want you all to take a few minutes to jot down party ideas with those around you. Think about what the perfect welcome party for our prince and princess would be," Rapunzel says. "We don't have much time to plan, I'm afraid. The royal court has next weekend available, so the headmistress has granted us permission to host the party then."

"One week?" Tessa cries. "There's no way we can get a suitable band to play on such short notice. Gnome-More books up months in advance. And how will we have time to order fine tablecloths and china?"

"No worries," AG interrupts. "Raz and I are going to her castle this weekend to pick out some for us to borrow. We'll bring back everything we need."

"Just the two of you?" Tessa says weakly, and AG nods. "I usually pick out linens for the group. I could come. It will be too much to carry them all yourself."

"You're too kind, Tessa, but that's what the Pegasus coach is for," Rapunzel says.

"What about a menu?" Tessa sounds desperate as she consults her scroll. "Little Miss Muffet's Bakery is so hot right now. She could do little quiches and tea sandwiches and—"

"We're using Pattycakes," Rapunzel says. "AG went there with her mother and said they make the best cinnamon rolls for dessert. We've also decided to skip the tea sandwiches. They're pretty, but no one eats them."

"Fried chicken is the perfect picnic food," AG says, and a few RLWs nod.

"I love fried chicken," says Maxine, licking her lips.

"Fried chicken?" Raza pouts. "But we have to eat it *with our hands*."

"Exactly!" Rapunzel cheers. "Headmistress Flora loves AG's ideas of making the party feel fun rather than stuffy. There will be outdoor games and magic carpet racing and dancing too."

Tessa stares at AG with a look bordering on contempt. "Sounds like you two already planned everything. I'm surprised we even needed an RLW meeting today."

AG frowns. "I didn't mean to step on anyone's toes."

"Nonsense," Rapunzel says. "There's still plenty for all the RLWs to do."

"We were thinking there could be a big tent, in case it rains, with picnic blankets scattered underneath containing picnic baskets with food," AG tells us. Everyone starts to get excited.

"This sounds like a great picnic," I agree. "It's not stuffy at all. Other than the tea." Tessa's frown deepens, which I love.

"Are you saying we're going to serve tea to royals sitting *on the ground*?" Raza looks horrified.

"Yes," Rapunzel says as if this part should be obvious. "Tea is still the perfect ending to any royal meal." AG nods. Raz places a stack of white napkins in front of us. "As are pretty napkins. Still a royal must." Tessa claps excitedly. "Why don't you work on turning these into a festive shape. We have over two hundred to do for next weekend, so we might as well get started. AG and I have actual tea with her mother this afternoon, so we may have to leave early."

Rapunzel drops a napkin in front of me, and I start to hack.

"Lavender scented," she says. "Gives the napkins a little something extra." She smiles at me cheekily. She knows I hate this stuff.

"I'm really good at folding napkins," says Tessa, folding a napkin in thirds.

"She is," Raza seconds, taking a napkin of her own. Tessa swipes it so that she has two.

"I won the RLW napkin-folding contest last spring and a golden napkin award from Princess Rose. It's hanging in my room."

I snort. "There's a golden napkin award?"

Ollie nudges me. "Don't make fun. I'm going for it this year." I stare at him worriedly, and he winks.

"Swans are so over," Tessa adds, eyeing AG's design. "Last year, my napkin was folded into a rose just beginning to bloom, and this year I'm thinking of making it a book with pages in honor of Princess Beauty."

"Lovely," Raza and Millie second.

Ollie makes his look like a pirate sail. Maxine's tongue is hanging out as she tries to fold her napkin like a square. I get frustrated and roll mine into a ball. AG quietly keeps working.

"AG!" Rapunzel cries, rushing over to see what AG created. One napkin is shaped like a braid, like Rapunzel's long hair; another is shaped like an apple for the Evil Queen; and the third is somehow transformed into a wolf or some sort of hairy animal. Maybe her dad? "Those are stunning! Everyone look at Allison Grace's napkins! These are the epitome of grace and beauty. AG? Why don't you teach us your style, and we'll copy it for the tea." She walks to the other end of the table to discuss silverware.

Tessa smiles at AG. "Wow, aren't you the perfect RLW already! We're lucky you joined."

"We are?" Raza says, and I hear what sounds like someone's foot being stomped on. "I thought she was making us mad."

This can't be good.

"I'm just trying to help," AG says, scratching her neck suddenly. She starts to scratch her hands too.

"Ignore them. They're a little too into being RLWs," I tell AG. "And napkin folding."

"And that is why you don't belong in this group, Gilly," Tessa snaps. "Napkins are important! AG could tell you that. She's a *real* princess. As a matter of fact, maybe we should start serving her as well." She stands up and bows to AG, who gapes.

"Tessa, you don't have to bow," AG says, scratching her right elbow. She's scratching so hard she's starting to make a red mark and her eyes are brimming with tears. "I just want to be part of the club. I've never been in a club before. That's all."

"Part of the club or president?" Tessa rips off her RLW president button. "Maybe you want this too." She tosses it across the table to AG.

"That's enough, Tessa," I say, but Tessa isn't looking at me. Her face has changed, and she suddenly looks concerned. She points to AG, but no words come out of her mouth.

"What's happening to your arm?" Tessa asks.

We all turn to AG, who looks down in horror. Her pale arm is suddenly growing hair at an alarming rate, almost as if... AG slaps her arm hard and the hair recedes for a split second, then starts to grow back.

"It's happening to your other arm now too," Raza points out.

AG laughs awkwardly. "Must have been that planting spell I tried in Fern Woodland's class. I should go talk to her. If you excuse me..." With a curtsy, she exits quickly.

"What was that about?" Maxine asks.

"I don't know." All I know is that AG's clearly upset. "If you'll excuse me." I motion to Maxine. "Come on."

By the time we get out of the classroom, AG is long gone

and the hall is empty. Before we can figure out which way to go, we hear a growl.

"It came from this way!" Maxine points to a hallway to her right. We hurry down it, and a creature galloping on all fours rushes past us. It's wearing our school uniform.

AG?

The creature bursts through an exit leading to the Pegasus stables. We quickly follow, stopping short when we reach the Pegasus corrals. The Pegasi have flattened themselves against the barn wall. Now I see why: a half-girl half-beast is cowering in the opposite corner.

Allison Grace's hands are covered in dark-brown fur. Her head has sprouted horns, and her back is hunched and twice its normal size, shredding what remains of her uniform jumper. Her eyes are now yellow, and fur has taken over her cheeks and chin. She opens her mouth, revealing sharp fangs. AG lets out a growl so deep I could swear I'm standing in front of Professor Wolfington.

"Don't look at me! I'm hideous!" AG says in a gravelly voice. She sounds surprisingly more human than beast. "Did anyone see me? Were you followed?" She claws at the walls of the barn, leaving scratch marks. "I can't let anyone see

me like this! Especially not Tessa and Raza. If they knew—
Aaaooooh!" She covers her face with her furry hands.

"Stop howling!" I rush over. She recoils in horror.
"Someone will hear you."

Interesting. Unlike Wolfington, who is menacing when
he's in wolf form, AG seems to only change in appearance.
On the inside, she's still a frightened girl.

"Oh, who am I kidding? They saw the fur on my arms.
They know. They're all going to know now! Once they realize
they can make me turn by upsetting me, they'll start making
me transform all the time!" She wipes her snout. "Once
Father knows I'm being made fun of, he'll make us move
again. I'll be back to homeschooling in the castle! Do you
have any idea how boring it is to do group projects when
your only choice of partner is Mother, Father, or servants?"

"Pretty boring." I sit a few feet away from her. Maxine
comes and does the same. "But you don't have to hide, AG.
FTRS is awesome because it accepts everyone. We have
all type of students here—trolls, ogres, fairies, pixies, mer-
people. No one is going to judge you because of the way
you look. We don't care that you're half…um…" Is there a
politically correct way to call her a beast?

"Half-beast?" AG supplies. "I really like you Gilly, but let's be honest: no one wants to be friends with a princess who looks like a wolf! Royalty shouldn't look this way, even if I was born with this condition. Father thinks it has something to do with the curse Stiltskin placed on him, which is why he's been on the hunt to find him for years. Once I turn, it takes me a half hour to turn back—*if* I calm down. And how can I calm down when I'm upset? If Father could reverse this curse, I wouldn't have to deal with this! A princess should be beautiful and delicate and not have claws instead of nails! I want to be normal like everyone else."

"What's so great about being normal?" I ask. "I feel like it's the things that make us different that people remember."

"No, those are the things people make fun of," AG sniffs.

"Don't give them a chance to make fun," I insist. "Own your beast side." AG stops panting and looks at me oddly. "If you're all 'Yeah, I'm a beast who could cut off your arm. What are you going to do about it?' they'll think you're cool."

"I already think your secret identity is cool!" says Maxine. "If you want to roam the forest, no one bothers you. If you want to hang out with animals, you can become one. If you want to jump high or be fast or scare someone, you can do that too! If you ask me, being part beast is a gift." AG doesn't say anything. Maybe we are getting through to her.

"It's like you have magic at your fingertips," I add. "The rest of us have to use a wand or cast a spell if we want to become something different. You have the power inside you. Why hide such an awesome talent?"

"You saw how Tessa and Raza acted when they saw my arm," AG says, her breath slowing. "They'd never understand that I can't control what I become. If they knew about my condition, they wouldn't want to hang out with me."

"Why would you want to hang out with people who would make fun of you for being unique?" I ask. AG seems stumped by this question. "Those aren't the kind of people I want to be friends with." I think of my own group of reform school pals. "I like being around people who like me for me, warts and all. People I can trust. Ones who have my back when I'm in a scrape and who tell me when I'm being all loosey-goosey like Humpty Dumpty." I point to AG. "You're acting like Humpty Dumpty."

AG turns away from us and faces the barn wall. "You don't understand what it's like! My mother is beautiful, and I'm…"

"An original," Maxine says firmly. "That's what my momma

calls me. Beauty comes from inside you. You just have to let it out like I have. I know I'm beautiful, and I don't let anyone tell me otherwise." She grins, and drool rolls down her chin.

"That's very sweet, Maxine, but I don't think being a beast is beautiful." AG looks at me. "And I don't think it makes me powerful either. It's a poison. I want my father to find Rumpelstiltskin and make this condition go away for good."

"That's a shame," I tell her. "Having a skill like yours could come in handy someday. I'd love to have you by my side in a battle."

"Princesses don't battle," AG says, but her argument is weak and she knows it.

"Your godmother does," I say. "I hear Snow is good in a battle too. A princess can be anything she sets her mind to… or so I'm told."

AG contemplates this, then gives me a wolfish smile. "I appreciate what you're both trying to do, but I don't agree." She holds up her hairy arms, which now look slightly less hairy. "I don't want to be this thing anymore." Her yellow eyes widen. "Can I trust you guys not to tell anyone what I really am?"

"We won't tell," I promise, and Maxine nods too.

"Thank you." She sighs. "Will you guys stay with me till I turn back?"

I squeeze her furry hand. "Of course." Maxine takes her other hand.

Then we sit there in silence, listening to the Pegasi eat hay and watching our friend till her hair starts to recede, her back, teeth, and nails shrink to regular size, and her eyes turn back to their regular color.

"I'm a princess again," AG says, sighing with relief.

I just smile, holding my tongue instead of telling her what I really think—that Allison Grace will always be a princess, no matter what form she's in.

CHAPTER 9

I Read You Like an Open Book

Jax is waiting for me when I get out of my Hexing and Healing Potions class, and he doesn't look happy.

"What did you and Jack talk about yesterday?" A flash of lightning through a stained glass window highlights Jax's already-dark expression. The weather has delayed this afternoon's magic carpet racing scrimmage between the girls' and boys' dorms.

"How about 'Hey, Gilly! Did you figure out how to counter-hex an angry court magician on a power trip in class?'" I ask.

"Or you could say, 'Hey, Jax! Sorry I ran out of lunch with Jack yesterday and totally ignored my best friend,'" Jax counters. "You were being jerky."

"You're the one who was jerky!" I insist.

Jax stops short. "I was a jerk? *I* was a jerk? You were the one siding with that beanstalk-bragging liar! How can you stand him?"

Now it's my turn to stop short. A pack of pixies flies into my back; then they grumble about my lack of etiquette and keep flying down the hall. "He's nice! And I didn't *side* with him. I agreed with him. There's a difference, and you'd know that if you tried to understand the situation from our point of view!"

"*Our* point of view?" Jax repeats as a roll of thunder makes the ground shake.

Jocelyn whistles as she pushes between the two of us and keeps going. "Someone's jealous," she sings.

Does she mean Jax? Jax is a royal. They don't get jealous. Do they? Sure, I've made a new friend, but Jax is still my closest. "Look, if you must know, I wanted to talk to him about Anna."

"You told him about Anna?" Jax thunders along with the thunder outside. People look at us.

I pull Jax into an alcove. We stand in front of a window that is getting pelted with raindrops. "Yes, Anna!" Jax starts to protest. "He's seen her with Stiltskin! He told me she seemed against the little troll, not with him. Jack thinks she wants to leave, but Stiltskin won't let her."

Jax's eyes spark with a look I don't understand. "Where? When? How does he know it's actually Anna? And what makes him think she's changed her mind about being in the Stiltskin Squad? You keep forgetting she left you standing here crying while she jumped on his magic cooking ladle and flew out of here."

I smart at the reminder. "Maybe she's realized she was wrong to trust him. Jack said Anna tried to stop Stiltskin from imprisoning his mom."

"And he just happens to know this girl was your sister?" Jax snorts. "How would he remember her name? He's lying!"

"He's not," I say, flustered. "Why would he lie about that? I need to rescue her. Now."

Jax doesn't look moved at all. "So let me guess." He folds his arms across his chest. "You're going to bust out of school with your new best friend, Jack, on a hunch and attempt to save everyone even though I've told you it's a bad idea because you have no idea where the troll is and what he's capable of. Am I right?"

Now I fold my arms across my chest too. "No." Jax looks at me as lightning lights up the alcove. "Okay, yes, but we haven't figured out the details yet."

"Gilly!" Jax throws his hands up. "This is a bad idea, and you know it. You have nothing to go on, and you're trusting this total stranger. I won't let you do this."

"Won't let me? Well, excuse me, Your Royal Highness." Jax narrows his eyes at me. "But I didn't ask the royal court's permission. I'm my own person, and if I want to go after Anna with Jack, I will. You don't control me."

"I'm not trying to control you! I'm just saying that this is a fool's errand, and you could screw things up for the whole investigation the royal court has going. My sister didn't see me for years when I went undercover, but even now, she wouldn't put FTRS before the needs of the whole kingdom." He stares fiercely at me. "Something isn't right with that kid. You are falling for his charade because he somehow knows Anna's name. It makes me wonder whether I should even trust *you* anymore."

I wince. Somehow our fight just went from kind of bad to really bad. "I'm not sure I trust you either." People in the nearby hall stop and stare at us as I blink back hot tears.

"Fine!" Jax shouts over the thunder. "But you're on your own! I'm not coming with you!"

"Fine!" I snap.

Jax is already walking toward a winding staircase that appears in front of where we're standing. I watch the staircase till it disappears and wonder if my friendship with Jax just went along with it.

"Show's over," I say and push through the students who stopped to watch our fight.

I walk quickly to the library and bite back tears. How could I have forgotten about the whole Jax-being-separated-from-his-family-because-he-went-undercover thing? Even so, Jax doesn't understand what I'm going through. He and Rapunzel are *royals*. The royal court would never have let them run off with a villain. Anna is a cobbler's daughter and an FTRS dropout. Jack's mom is a commoner. The royal court doesn't care about them. The only ones who do are us.

I push open the library doors.

"Gilly!" Beauty says, greeting me warmly. "Back to do more research on your school project? Sebastian told me they're due next week."

Spoken like a true mother.

"Yes." I try to hide the unhappiness in my voice. I glance up at the darkened top floor of the library and the atrium ceiling, which is almost pitch-black with the storm whipping up outside. "I had some time between classes, so I thought I'd look around."

Beauty hugs the books she's holding to her chest and smiles. "Wonderful! A rainy afternoon is the perfect time to cozy up in the library. I could read for hours in this weather. I'm sure Sebastian told you what we discussed," she adds. "Under the circumstances, gaining an interview with Anna for your project is not possible, and it won't affect your grade." I feel momentarily hopeful again. "As for the rest of your family, since you haven't gotten a weekend pass yet, you may have to interview them through Miri. We can send a mirror to their boot so you can converse. Isn't that great?"

I know the princess went to bat for me, and I'm grateful. I just still can't believe the Beast won't let me go home for a weekend.

Beauty leads me to one of the magical librarian stations as a clap of thunder rattles the windows. "This is Helga." She motions to the aging fairy with the white hair and the scowl.

"She can help you find anything you need. Have fun!" Beauty delicately picks up the bottom of her skirt so it doesn't trail and heads into a library stack.

"Thanks!" I say and approach Helga. The fairy is considerably older than Kayla's family and her wings are a bit droopy—like her skin, which looks like a dried-up prune. She's going to be tough to crack. "Hi there. My professor told me to find a book on"—I lower my voice so Beauty can't hear me—"Rumpelstiltskin and his origin story. Could you help me find some titles?"

Helga purses her withered lips. "Rumpelstiltskin?" She lets his name hang there.

"Yes. It's for a history assignment from Professor Wolfington," I lie. "'Knowing a villain is the best way not to become a villain,' he always says." I laugh nervously.

Helga wands the scroll in front of her, and a glittery list of books pops up. I strain to see the names, but she turns the scroll away so I can't see.

"I've got one on Enchantasia history." She lifts a large dark-green book titled *A Kingdom United* from below the counter. The front page flies open and a small weed begins to grow out of the pages. She taps her wand again quickly, and the weed disappears. "Forgot to disarm this book before I showed it to you." She whispers a few words that I can't quite make out. "There! Now you can take this one out and not have it growing in your dorm room. Enchantasia is famed for its ivy growing."

"I didn't know that." I'm trying to make conversation. (I really didn't know that.)

Helga shakes her head. "Fast-growing ivy is a nasty problem to have. A child last week almost got choked by her own book vines." She goes to hand me the book, then takes it back. "Name?"

I smile again. "Gillian Cobbler."

She consults her list. "You don't have any overdue books—*yet*. You can take this out, but Stiltskin books need permission from the headmistress."

"Oh, I already have permission," I say, feeling like a squeaky spinning wheel. "I wouldn't ask if I didn't."

Helga glares at me. "I need it in writing."

"I have it here somewhere." If I pretend to rummage around in my sack, maybe she'll assume I'm telling the truth. "I know I had it this morning. Which book did I put it in? Did I leave it in *Spelling 101*? Or *Ferns: Our Greatest Allies*?

Let's see… Oh, I don't know where I put it." I sound aghast. "But I do have one."

"Uh-huh," Helga says, looking doubtful. "Can't give you a book without the note."

Grrr…

"Not sure we even have one. The master took all the books we had on that man and kept them in his private study. He's been studying Rumpelstiltskin for years."

Prince Sebastian. *Great.* The one person at this school who might know what I need to know about Rumpelstiltskin would never share that info with me. Now what?

Helga glances up at the darkened floor for a spilt second, sees me staring, and looks away. "So like I said, no note, no book, not that there even is a book to take out."

I lean over the counter to see if she's telling the truth. "Are you sure? There has to be one book on him here. Every villain has a beginning, don't they?"

Helga stares at me, and I stare back again. "Not all of them. Some are born evil."

"Even so, they'd have a story or a book," I press. "I doubt Beauty would stock a library as magnificent as this without any books on one of the greatest villains in our kingdom. The prince can't keep them all! As a magical librarian, I doubt you'd allow that." I smile serenely.

Helga glowers. "There is one, but it's already checked out: *Rumpelstiltskin: The Man vs. the Myth*."

I frown. "Who has it out?"

"I'm not at liberty to say."

"Can I be put on a wait list?" I ask impatiently.

She taps the quill in her other hand. "I'll ask." We hear a crash from somewhere in the stacks.

"Helga? Can you help me?" Beauty calls.

Helga sighs. "She balances too many books in her hands. You'll have to wait till I get back." Helga flutters away at the slowest speed imaginable.

I wait till she's gone before I jump over her desk and pick up her wand. Quickly tapping the scroll, I see the Rumpelstiltskin title again and look to see who has it checked out. Fiddlesticks, it says *Classified!* I hear another crash and tap the scroll again, making the title disappear.

"Now what?" I ask Wilson, who is hanging out in my pocket. "How can a library this big only have one book on Stiltskin? I can't even order one from the village because they'd flag it." I bang the wand against the library desk in frustration. "All I want to do is read a book about Rumpelstiltskin so I can help my sister and all the other missing kids. If I did, I know I'd be smart enough to figure out what he's after and why!"

Wilson starts to squeak madly, and I look at the desk, which is starting to glow orange. I back away, wondering if I've set off some sort of alarm, but no sound comes. Instead, a small gold book with worn silver pages materializes in front of us. There are red scratch marks on the cover, along with what appears to be a bite out of the top corner of the book. I read the title: *Curses and Dark Deeds: The Rumpelstiltskin Legend.* That wasn't the title Helga mentioned. Hmm....

I lunge for the book, and Wilson nips me.

"Ouch!" I whisper, wishing I could yell. Wilson starts squeaking crazily. I calm down and try to understand him. "You're worried that this book just showed up when I mentioned needing one. And you think I shouldn't read it." Wilson stops squeaking. "But what if the book showed up because it *wants* me to help Anna." Wilson is quiet. "If it lets me pick it up, then I'm meant to have it. Why else would a book that isn't even in the library catalog just appear?"

"I've got to help a girl fill out a book request sheet," I hear Helga croak. "Otherwise I would be happy to help shelve more books." Helga is coming back.

My heart starts to beat faster, and my palms begin to sweat as that familiar feeling of thieving comes over me. It feels like that brief high I'd get when I pinched something I needed and no one saw. I stare at the book again. I could read it tonight and bring it back tomorrow. If it's not in the library catalog, no one will even notice it's missing. I glance quickly around the library. There's no sign of Beauty or other fairy librarians. I reach out slowly and touch the book jacket. If the book is alarmed, it will probably yell at me or spring to life. Nothing happens, so I test the waters further by throwing open the book flap. I jump back and waiting for a ghostly Stiltskin to pop out and yell at me. Nothing happens.

I give the surrounding area one last glance, then grab the book and drop it into my book bag, which I quickly tie together and sling onto my back. Then I hurry to the door.

"Gilly?" I stop short and turn around.

It's Beauty. "Did you find everything you need already?"

"Yes, I did. Thanks!" A flash of lightning makes me jump. With that, I rush to the library exit. An alarm doesn't go off.

This is meant to be. I can feel it. The Rumpelstiltskin clues I need are finally within my reach.

CHAPTER 10

Read No Evil

I spend the majority of the afternoon alone in my room with Wilson, Peaches, and the book, which is still in my bag. I need to get it back to the library before anyone knows it's missing. But if Helga realized it was gone, she would have come calling for it by now. I *think*.

Our dorm mirror, which Maxine bedazzled with jewels she's found (not stolen, I hope), starts to glow yellow, then blue.

"Good afternoon, Fairy Tale Reform School!" Flora's voice booms over the magical loudspeaker system. "Due to the weather, the magic carpet racing scrimmage has been canceled for today." Groans can be heard throughout the girls' dorms. "Dinner will be served at five o'clock in the cafeteria where we are testing out several recipes for Monday's welcome tea for our new teachers. Please vote on your favorite dessert: Happily Brownie After Sundae or Tale as Old as Tapioca Pudding. Enjoy the rest of your afternoon, and remember: 'Be good' is not a saying. It's a way of life!"

I stare at my book bag again. *Open the book*, a voice inside me seems to shout.

Quack!

Peaches waddles over as if she hears my thoughts. Winston crawls from my desk to my bed and plops down on my right kneecap. They're both staring at me suspiciously, and I didn't even take the book out of my bag yet.

"Are you guys hungry?" I reach into my desk drawer and pull out some cheese for Winston and a quill for Peaches. She loves chomping on those. But neither of them move. Winston squeaks madly at Peaches, and Peaches quacks at Winston. Then she starts to cough.

"What did you eat now?" I cry, jumping up to find the ELF Cleaning Spray.

Peaches coughs up something small and gold. "It's Jack's mirror! And in one piece." I pick it up. "When did you eat this again?" Peaches quacks madly and tries to steal the mirror back. I put it up high on my dresser and grab my book bag.

The last thing I need is Peaches getting vindictive and eating the library book next. I sit down on my bed again and take the book out of the bag, preparing to open the first page.

Winston jumps on the book, and Peaches starts snapping at my fingers. Then she starts to cough again. I do not want the duck throwing up on the book!

"Guys, quit it, or you're going back in the Magical Fairy Pets cages!" That makes them quiet. "I didn't steal the book," I add, guilt taking over me. "I *borrowed* it. And since it's here, I might as well read it, right?" I turn to the first page and read the inscription:

The reader embarks on this history of Rumpelstiltskin at his or her own risk.

What does that mean?

I turn the page again, and my dorm room door bursts open.

"Gilly, want to have dinner with us?" Kayla asks cheerfully. "Mother is making fairy cakes, and her blueberry one tastes more like dessert than dinner, so I thought you'd like—*Oh!*" She spots the book, sees the name Rumpelstiltskin written in big, black letters, and begins to stutter. "Wh-where did you get that? *Why* do you have that? What are you doing?"

I try to hide the book, but Peaches nips me again and Winston starts chittering. "I borrowed it from the library."

Kayla's brow furrows. "Borrowed or stole?"

We stare at each other for a moment. "Kind of both," I say meekly.

Kayla's wings pop out of her back. "What if that book comes alive?" she says, panicking. "What if Rumpelstiltskin shows up in this room? What if…what if…the book is evil?" Her amber eyes widen.

I jump up and cover her mouth before Miri hears her. "I won't let it do anything evil. Anna is in danger. I just need to figure out where she is so Jack and I can rescue her."

Kayla cocks her head. "Do you mean Jack or Jax?"

"Jack." I look away. "Jax and I aren't talking."

"And now you and Jack are teaming up?" Kayla asks. "Why? You barely know him."

"He's seen Anna." Kayla's mouth opens slightly. "Back when Stiltskin took his mom. He said she's disenchanted with Stiltskin. Just like I hoped she'd become! Between what Jack's seen and what I can find out in this book, maybe we have a chance of getting our families back and convincing all the other kids to leave him too."

"So you thought you could figure this out with a book you're not even allowed to take out?" she asks.

I look away again.

"And you were going to do all this without your friends' help? Gilly, come on! You aren't thinking straight! Don't be foolish. This book could be full of lies. Do you even know who wrote it? A villain or a fairy? Or a royal? That changes everything. You heard what Beauty said in our library class—if you can't trust the author of the book, you have to wonder whether you can trust the content inside it."

"I'll be careful," I promise. "I haven't even gotten past the first page yet."

"You're not listening to me." Kayla is growing impatient. "If the book appeared when you needed it and allowed itself to leave the library, then it *wanted* to leave the library!"

"What are you talking about?" I ask. Kayla isn't making any sense.

She puts one delicate hand on her right hip. "Didn't you pay attention in class? Beauty said villain books can't leave the library without permission because they try to control their reader by feeding them false information. Only a fairy is strong enough to withstand such impulses—most of the time. It's why fairies protect villain books in the first place. If this book showed itself to you when you went looking for it, it can't be trusted."

"Then this must not be an actual villain book, because I'm not a fairy and it let me pick it up," I counter. "And besides, a book doesn't have feelings." I pat the book, and it starts to glow. Peaches quacks frantically. I frown. "It wasn't glowing like that before."

Kayla's eyes narrow. "See?" She begins backing away from the book. "Don't open that book! It looks familiar to me. I'm not sure why, but you shouldn't open it. You have to tell the teachers what happened."

I huff. "You're being ridiculous! Maybe this book trusts me to do the right thing, and that's why it showed itself when I needed it to. Maybe it knows Jack and I are the ones meant to find Rumpelstiltskin."

Kayla crosses her arms. "Rumpelstiltskin has been around a long time. Don't you think if it only took two kids to stop him, someone would have already? Trust us. *We*—your friends, teachers, family—want to help Anna. You just have to give us time to figure out what to do."

"Everyone keeps saying that, but no one is doing anything!" I feel suddenly desperate. "If Anna has decided to be good again, then I have to get to her before she changes her mind." I look at the book again. "I'm opening it."

"Don't!" Kayla whips out her training wand and tries to zap the book from me. "Let me show it to Mother first!" I hold it tighter as Kayla continues to spell me. Peaches and Winston are squawking madly, and I jump up and try to run out of the room so she can't stop me. That's when I trip. The book goes flying across the room, opening to a page in the middle of the book. Kayla gasps as the book's narrator speaks in a smooth, feminine voice.

Ten years before the Troll War, Rumpelstiltskin made an unlikely alliance with the one person he swore he'd never befriend: Alva of Elendale. Even though she had betrayed him more than once, Rumpelstiltskin and Alva made beautiful music together. It is said she was his one true love. Others said Alva used the trickster to do her dirty work in the fairy kingdom. The evil fairy and the deal maker created an unlikely alliance and worked tirelessly to find the ingredients needed to complete their biggest spell yet: one that would send them back to the past so they could change their futures.

The book slams shut with a bang, and the glowing stops. The four of us—the fairy pets included—stare at the book on the floor in shock.

"That voice sounded somewhat familiar." Kayla makes a face. "And Alva dated Rumpelstiltskin? Eww."

"That's what you got out of that?" I tap the book to see if it will zap me. I'm able to pick it up, no problem. "Beautiful music together—do you think that is why he's looking for music? Hayley mentioned that in her Pegasus Post."

"Making beautiful music and actual music are two different things, aren't they?" Kayla asks. "Didn't her post also mention a book? What if he's looking for this one?" Her face darkens. "And my mother was talking about a book too. You heard her the other night."

I feel a little queasy. "It can't be the same book." Can it? Is this the book Rumpelstiltskin is looking for? Or Kayla's mother? Why did the book find me? "What do you think the book meant about finding a way to the past? People can't revisit their past. Can they?"

"I don't think so. The book must be lying to you." Kayla yanks the book from me. "I'm taking this to Mother. She'll know what to do."

"No! You can't! I'll get in trouble." I try to grab the book again, and Peaches starts choking.

The duck opens her beak, and the mirror drops out

again, clattering to the floor. It starts to glow, the glass on the mirror swirling like it does when Miri visits.

"Hide the book," I tell Kayla.

Kayla holds the book behind her back, and we wait for Miri. Instead, the purple mist on the glass fades away, and a picture slowly comes into view. Kayla, Peaches, Wilson and I lean in for a closer look. People are working on some sort of assembly line. They're kids! Kids I recognize!

A girl with dark-brown hair lifts a heavy parcel and carries it to another boy, both of them stumbling slightly under the weight. The girl is crying. I can't hear what they're saying, but I can see the boy yelling at the girl. Some of the other kids are crying too. The girl turns toward the mirror.

"Oh my God! That's Anna!" I pick up the mirror.

"What's she carrying?" Kayla asks as we watch the kids move large parcels that look like hay bales. The picture isn't crystal clear, so it's hard to tell. Two more kids start yelling at Anna now too. "Is that straw?"

"I think so." I look for clues as to where they are. I don't see Jack's mom, not that I know what she looks like, or a cow. All I see is the Stiltskin Squad and miles and miles of blue sky. The ground is a white, fluffy mist. Are they on a mountaintop?

Suddenly, our view is blocked by a smaller kid. He's got his back to us, but I notice his stringy hair, patterned jacket, and bright-green pants. He starts motioning wildly to Anna, and she bursts into tears and runs out of the frame. That's when the kid turns around.

He's no kid.

Rumpelstiltskin smiles cunningly, like he sees us. Then he waves his hand, and the mirror's image fades to black.

"No!" I shake the mirror. Anna was so close. So close!

Kayla looks at me. "We are taking this book to Mother. *Now.*"

CHAPTER 11

Fairy Tales

I follow Kayla through the castle, my breath coming fast. Jack was telling the truth. Anna is being bullied by Stiltskin! My instincts were right: Anna is miserable and wants to come home.

We race past the pumpkin patch and the vegetable garden and beyond the magic carpet racetrack into a woodsy area close to the Hollow Woods. In the distance, I can see Prince Sebastian and Beauty's castle. I don't see a fairy hut anywhere.

Kayla stops near a cluster of trees. "Ready?" she asks.

I look around. "Ready for what? Where's your house?" Instead of answering me, Kayla blows something glittery in my face. I start to cough as the scent of rosemary and lavender overwhelms me. My hands start to glow, moving from my fingers all the way to my feet. My body starts to tingle as the trees in front of me swirl like the mirror in my hands.

Kayla grabs my arm, and then I'm falling, falling, falling. Suddenly, I stop. My hands aren't tingling. I'm still holding the mirror. My arms aren't glowing. *Holy gingerbread!* I stare up at the tree I was just standing next to. It looks about a hundred feet tall! So do the blades of grass that surround us! We are standing at the base of the tree trunk, and somehow I'm now…

"Six inches tall," Kayla says. "Cool, huh?"

Even the book and the mirror have shrunk!

Kayla knocks on the tree trunk, and a small door appears. "I didn't tell you about the shrinking part because it freaks people out. You should have seen Headmistress Flora the first time she visited!" Kayla laughs. The door opens, and Kayla leads me inside a sitting area. "The secrecy is for our own protection after all that happened with You-Know-Who. Fairies can be full size or small, and for the time being, we've kept our house tiny. We save a lot on rent this way too. Mother?" Kayla calls. "I'm home! I brought Gilly."

Kayla leads me through the house, where I pass doors marked with signs that say Fairy Garden, Herb Room, and

Flying Training Room. As we near the kitchen, I smell the blueberry fairy cake Kayla was talking about earlier. Kayla's mom is floating around the kitchen as pots whisk themselves. I watch as she drops a handful of spices into a pot, and it bubbles over. Then her mom wands the pot, and the bubbling ceases. Sensing me, she turns around. Her eyes are the same amber shade as Kayla's.

"Gillian," she says, pulling me in for an embrace. "I'm so glad you could join us for supper. How are you doing, dear?"

"I'm fine," I say in surprise. Kayla's right—it's as if her mother doesn't remember me helping her out of the forest the other night at all. A mother would have mentioned that sort of thing. "Thank you for having me, Ms...."

"Please, call me Angelina." She stands back and looks at me. "How are you holding up? Are you sleeping okay? Eating? Consumed with revenge?" I blink in surprise. "Kayla told me about your sister Anna joining the Stiltskin Squad. I can only imagine what you're feeling—probably a lot like Kayla did without us. Not that I know or remember much." She smiles. "But you will get through this test. That's all it is, really. A test. We take many of them in life. Let's get you fed, and we'll talk all about it."

"Thank you," I say, slightly embarrassed by the fuss. My mind is still on the book and what it could mean.

"What's wrong, dear?" Kayla's mom can read me well. Fairies usually do. "Did your shrinking spell go okay?" She touches my ears. "Sometimes the ears get misshapen during the shrinking process, and you wind up with ears that look like mine." She motions to her pointy lobes. "But yours look fine! They could use some earrings to liven up this dull uniform though." She studies my face for a second. "How do you feel about silver half-moons?"

"Mother," Kayla says impatiently. "There's no time for ear piercing." She motions for me to take the book out. I place it on the table. "When I got to Gilly's room, she was reading *this*. Do you recognize this book? Is it the one you keep talking about? It looks sort of familiar to me."

Kayla's mom's smile vanishes.

Immediately, her shoulders droop, and the wooden spoon in her left hand clatters to the floor. It's like she'll do anything to get away from us. She looks wildly for an exit, then flattens herself like a gingerbread man against the closed kitchen door. She seems unable to even speak, let alone scream. Then she starts to convulse. Kayla and I look at each other in alarm.

"Mother!" Kayla cries. "Gilly, get the book out of her sight."

I try to grab it but feel a zap. The book is refusing to move again. Instead, its pages flutter open, whipping by at light speed even as the book whispers words and phrases I don't understand.

Kayla's mom is near tears as she continues to shake violently. Kayla and I try everything to get the book to stop, but no matter what we do, the book vanquishes the distractions.

Finally, Kayla's mom grabs her own wand from the counter and points it at the book. Her arm is shaking, but her voice is clear. "Finireto!" she shouts, and the book closes. The glowing ceases, the voices stop, and the book becomes just a book once more. Kayla scoops it up and tosses it through the doorway into the living room. Her mom sinks to the kitchen floor, mumbling the same thing over and over.

"I remember! He knew, he knew! I remember!" she repeats again and again.

"I think she's having some sort of breakthrough," Kayla tells me. "I need to get my sisters and Professor Harlow. Can you stay with her?"

"Of course." I lean down by Kayla's mom. Her pointy, pale ears are turning a vibrant shade of pink. Her normally amber eyes are muddy black as if she's been possessed. "Angelina?" I try. "You're okay. Kayla is getting your other daughters." She keeps mumbling. "And Professor Harlow. Remember the Evil Queen?" She stops and looks at me. "The book is gone. You don't have to ever see it again."

Angelina grabs my wrists hard. "That book is mine. I wrote it!" Any trace of kindness on her face is gone, replaced with something much darker. "It will always follow me because it holds the truth about him, and I'm the fairy tasked with recording it. He can't know it's here. Where did you find it?"

"He?" I'm confused. It dawns on me. "Do you mean Rumpelstiltskin?"

"Don't say his name!" She presses harder, and it hurts. "Where did you find that book?"

"It was in the library," I say, wincing.

"Impossible!" Angelina's face is racked with pain. "Where did you get it? I haven't seen it since before he cursed me. How did you open it?"

"Open it? It's a book," I remind her as she yanks harder, leaving nail marks on my skin.

"That book can only be opened by fairies! It would never be

in a reform school library, unless"—her face softens slightly—"someone brought it here to be opened. Who gave it to you?"

"It just appeared!" I insist.

She lets go of my wrists. "And it let you see what I had written, like it once did for Alva?" I nod, and her face darkens again. "Alva was evil. Are you?"

"No! I'm not!" My voice is sure and clear. "I'm on the good side." I move backward to avoid her grasp.

She studies me closely. "I see. Then how…" She looks upward. "Why would the book trust you? It's never trusted anyone but me and Alva before. And him. He took it from me with her help." Her breathing comes faster now again. "Maybe he knows he needs me to finish his story and tell him how it ends."

She's not making any sense. I grab a cloth from the stove handle and dab her sweaty forehead. "You say you wrote his villain story?" I'm afraid to say his name in her presence.

"Don't you understand, child?" Angelina closes her eyes as if the memory is too much to bear. "Villain stories are written by fairies that foresee potential futures. The future is a hard thing to predict, but my family has been blessed—or cursed—with the gift to view glimpses." She opens her eyes.

"He knew I had that gift, so he nurtured it, and I fell for his promises, like many had before. I could see his future, and I foolishly told him what I saw. I wrote it all down in that book!" Her voice grows angry again.

"And then when something I wrote down made him upset, he trapped me in the same wood as those book pages, deep in the fairy forest. He wanted no one to see that book or its theories, so he hid me away, kidnapping Kayla and making her work with Gottie for my girls' and my freedom. But now I'm back, and so is that book." Her lower lip trembles. "If he knows the book is here, he may already be too. He wants to know the ending. And if he doesn't like it, he'll expect me to change it." She closes her eyes. "He never understood it doesn't work that way."

If he were here, we'd know, wouldn't we? I need to keep her calm till help arrives.

"The book must have sensed Kayla's presence, which is why it opened," I realize. "It only read us one paragraph, and we didn't understand a word of it. Something about him and Alva?" Angelina's eyes flutter closed again. "It said they make music together, which seems pretty far-fetched. His speaking voice is dreadful. There is no way he can carry a tune."

A look of recognition comes over Angelina's face just as Professor Harlow bursts through the door with her wand illuminated. Kayla, Jocelyn, Emma Rose, and Brooke Lynn are right behind her. Headmistress Flora is last, her ears pointy and bright green. A mass shrinking spell seems to have many ramifications.

"I remember," Angelina tells the room. "I remember everything." The room is silent, giving her room to process what she's actually saying. "I was the one tasked with writing Rumpelstiltskin's villain book. When he liked my predictions, he was happy. But when he wasn't pleased with the direction of things, he got angry. I came to a part in the book that was frightening, and I didn't want to keep going."

Kayla reaches for her mother's hand.

"He didn't want me to stop writing, but I feared if I kept going, he'd learn the ingredients he needed for something... What was it?" Angelina thinks for a moment, and her eyes widen. "It was for a spell! A dark spell that would allow him to go back to the beginning of our kingdom, before Enchantasia or our royal courts ever took power." Her eyes slowly return to their eerie amber shade. "I couldn't allow that to happen, so I didn't want to know his ending. I refused to write anymore."

"Oh, Mother," Kayla says, near tears.

"Impossible." Harlow touches her right ear, which is pointy and twice its normal size. "I don't mean to contradict you, but are you sure your memory isn't muddy? Villains can't read their own books, and they certainly never know what fairy is in charge of their stories. Believe me, I've tried to find out who wrote mine, and no amount of threatening ever revealed the source."

"Rumpelstiltskin was too vain to allow his book to be written without him knowing the fairy who was doing the writing," Angelina explains. "I have no clue what deal he must have made to find out it was me, but once he knew, he visited me daily to see how my writing was going. I didn't trust him at first, but he finally wore me down with his generosity. He was always bringing us what we needed! Food, clothes, presents."

"Bribery works wonders," Harlow acknowledges.

Angelina's face flushes. "I am ashamed to say I liked the attention. Then, he became friendly with my girls, including Kayla, who was so little at the time." Her eyes grow teary as she turns to her daughter. "He was so fond of you. He made me believe I was his family. He told me he wanted what was best for me—to see me become Fairy Queen and rule the forest—and I foolishly believed his trickery."

"Just like Anna did," I say aloud.

"Until you stopped telling him his story." Flora fills in the details. "Do you remember what happened then?"

"Yes." Angelina covers her face with her hands, pulling her hand away from Kayla. "Once I wrote about the spell he was after, I became worried he would use it. His curse would destroy Enchantasia! So I stopped writing, and he became furious."

"Are you sure you have the spell right?" Harlow asks. "There is no magic that can rewind time. If there were, every villain would use it."

"There is such magic, but it is well hidden," Angelina explains. "I didn't want him to know the ingredients he needed to complete his spell, so I stalled. I told him I felt uncomfortable going further with the story because I had been breaking the fairy code of honor by letting him know his story. He became infuriated and vindictive. Soon, I barely recognized the man who used to feed Kayla her evening bottle."

"Gross," Kayla says.

Angelina looks up at us wearily. "He disappeared for a while, so I thought maybe he'd given up. Then he showed up and gave me an ultimatum. If I didn't finish the book, he would tell everyone that I had broken my fairy vow by sharing his story with him. I'd be banished from the fairy kingdom, and so would the girls. I knew I had no choice. I remember giving him the book with a false list of ingredients, and when he realized his spell wouldn't work, he made sure I was no longer a threat to him." She closed her eyes again. "Obviously he wants me to have the book back so I can finish the story."

"And you must," Harlow insists. "It's your fairy duty. But now, more than ever, we have to protect you and the book to make sure he doesn't ever see it."

"I can't." Angelina starts to shake again. "I don't want to know how it all ends."

"Well, we do!" Harlow snaps, getting angry. "You may hold the key to stopping him. You must start writing the book again and find out the ingredients he needs so we can make sure he doesn't get his hands on them."

"No!" Kayla cries. "If she finishes the book, he'll find her and torture her to tell him its secrets. It's too dangerous!"

Everyone begins to argue, and Angelina raises her hand for silence.

"Harlow is right. I must finish writing. We all need to know how his story progresses from here," Angelina whispers. "It's my duty. I already broke too many fairy promises as it is." She shakes her head and looks at me. "No wonder he broke my spell. He made it seem like it was part of your deal with him, but in truth, he needed me to finish his story. He always has an ulterior motive."

"Have you found out anything about this spell he needs to work on?" Flora asks.

"He knows he needs the music of true love to start unlocking it," she tells us. "And music usually involves an instrument. I know the one he seeks—a golden harp. The only one I know of is in Cloud City. If he has magic beans, he can reach it."

"He already has magic beans," I say worriedly. "We saw some in his office when he was at FTRS."

"Then he can reach the harp," Angelina says. "If he and his true love try to use it together, he'll have the first piece of his spell in place. When I was writing the book, I suspected his true love was Alva."

"That must be why he wanted to come to FTRS in the first place—to find Alva," Flora guesses. "But he's out of luck. She'll be doing no singing in her condition."

Harlow looks thoughtful. "If he wanted that book to get back to Angelina, it's curious that it showed itself to Gillian and found its way here." She tsks. "Careful, Cobbler. I suspect he knows he can play you."

"I've tricked him once," I say defiantly. "He can't play me." I think back to how I thought I saw Alva's finger move once. "How long do you think your magic will keep Alva trapped in stone?"

"Forever?" Harlow guesses. "That's my hope."

"Nothing is forever," Angelina says. "Not magic, not curses, not happily ever afters. If I complete the book—and I must—and he forces me to tell him the ending…"

I slump down against the wall next to her. I finish her thought. "Then he'll finish his spell, and Enchantasia as we know it will be done for."

"Not on my watch," Harlow says fiercely. She looks at us. "We should all be on alert. Rumpelstiltskin obviously has a plan, and I wouldn't be surprised if it is already in motion."

Happily Ever After Scrolls

Brought to you by FairyWeb—Enchantasia's

Number One News Source!

Welcome Tea for Prince Sebastian and Princess Beauty's Family to Be Held at Fairy Tale Reform School This Weekend!

by Beatrice Beez

According to the royal court's chief sorcerer, the weather should be perfect for Prince Sebastian and Princess Beauty's Fairy Tale Reform School welcoming this weekend! Reporters have been buzzing around FTRS all week to watch the staff ready what has been described as a "very simple" event for the newest staff members.

"Princes Sebastian and Princess Beauty aren't ones to make a big fuss about anything," says a palace insider. "It's why there was no fanfare when they arrived in Enchantasia in the first place. The pair and their young daughter, Allison Grace, are very shy and prefer to keep things low-key."

Low-key seems to be the approach the newest royal family has when it comes to everything. Instead of having a castle built on royal court palace grounds, the newest family chose to move into a pop-up castle on the grounds of Fairy Tale Reform School where their daughter attends classes. "No one can understand why they didn't send Allison Grace to Royal Academy like all the other royals," sniffs one insider. "Olivina has seen it as a huge snub."

The prince and princess have obviously paid no mind to the legendary fairy godmother's worries. "They're very protective of their daughter," says the source. And their pop-up castle seems permanent, as the family has added a playground and lovely garden to their property. Those who have seen inside the pop-up castle say it has all the amenities a regular castle would, from a ballroom to a grand kitchen. We wonder if either will get much use. The family is said to have kept to themselves a lot on weekends and usually spends a great deal of time indoors. "Strange, if you ask me," says the source. "Why wouldn't you show your daughter off?"

That's why this Welcome Tea brings so much excitement! Enchantasia can't wait to see the royal family mingling with other royals, village folk, and students alike! While Rapunzel, who runs FTRS's Royal Ladies-in-Waiting club, is in charge of the event and is said to be going with an unusual picnic theme, all the stops were still pulled out to get the venue ready. The Dwarf Police Squad has shiny new uniforms to wear as they patrol the school grounds for any sign of trouble. (There should be none. When's the last time anyone heard of a villain or Rumpelstiltskin lately?) China has been borrowed, oriental rugs have taken the place of picnic blankets, and fried chicken of all things is said to be on the menu. And tea, of course. "Fairy Tale Reform School is looking forward to hosting a lovely party for our newest faculty and their family," says school spokesmirror Miri. "A good time should be had by all."

Stay tuned for all the details and magical pictures from Prince Sebastian and Princess Beauty's Welcome Tea!

CHAPTER 12

The Welcome Party

I've never been to a fairy party, but I imagine this is what it would look like. The grounds of Fairy Tale Reform School are twinkling with hundreds of paper lanterns hanging from tree branches, floating on the lake, and lighting the path to a beautiful, blue tent. Inside the tent, members of the royal court are on hand to officially welcome Prince Sebastian, Beauty, and AG to Enchantasia.

Students from FTRS are dressed in their cleanest uniforms and shiniest shoes, while the Dwarf Police Squad patrols the lake to make sure there are no unwelcome visitors. The dwarves look sort of knightly in their flashy, new uniforms. With the sun dipping behind the lake and a sky ablaze with pinks and reds, I have to admit that FTRS looks even prettier than one of those fancy magical postcards.

And Rumpelstiltskin wants nothing more than to see this world I have grown to love wiped from existence.

"Stop worrying in public, Ms. Cobbler," Professor Harlow says as she sweeps by me in a gold gown that has a jewel-encrusted bodice. The look would be very fairy-tale princess if she wasn't also wearing a black cape. "Those frown lines will give you premature wrinkles."

"But…" I start to protest.

"No buts," Harlow says. "We've done a sweep of the grounds, and we've got those ridiculous dwarves here for extra protection. Angelina is safely hidden, and I've cast spells that will keep intruders from walking onto FTRS grounds this evening." She leans closer, practically wrapping me in her cape.

"Act normal. If he is looking for that book and watching us, we can't look frightened." I start to protest. "Drink chamomile tea with your friends, and calm down. There will be plenty of work to do tomorrow when this *fanfare* is over." She gives a look of disdain to a fairy flying balloons to the tent. Just as Harlow enters the party, Jax exits. I see him notice me, and I pretend to be fixing a paper lantern that looks crooked.

"Hey." Jax comes up beside me.

"Hey," I say back.

"Nice party," Jax says lamely. "Great decorations."

"Yeah. Beautiful lanterns." I hear crickets in the distance and someone tuning their violin. I have no clue what to say to my best friend right now.

Jax sighs. "Thief, this is silly. I hate fighting with you."

I drop the lantern. "I hate fighting with you too." I jab my finger at his frilly collar. "But you started it."

He jabs his finger at my poufy shoulder. "Me? You did!"

"No, you did!"

Jax puts up a hand to stop me. "Can we just forget this fight ever happened? I think we both said some things we wish we didn't."

"True." A group of partygoers carrying mini paper lanterns skip down the path past us. "I just can't stand the thought of you not trusting me."

"I *do* trust you," Jax insists. "It's him I don't." He nods in the direction of the castle, where Jack is lurking near an exit, looking around. I know that doorway he's near. It's the only exterior entrance to the dungeon. Hmm…

"I'm sure there is a perfectly reasonable explanation for

why he'd be down in the dungeon." I try to sound nonchalant. "Why don't we go ask him?"

Jack grins devilishly. "With pleasure."

The two of us approach Jack together. "Hey. What are you doing?"

Jack doesn't blink an eye. "I was in the dungeons. Why?"

"What were you doing down there?" Jax demands.

Jack rolls his eyes. "For the love of Grimm, what do you think I'm up to, Prince?" he asks Jax. "If you must know, I was bringing Raza and Tessa crumb cakes and tea."

"Ha!" I nudge Jax.

Jack looks at me strangely. "They're pretty upset about missing the welcome party since they helped plan it."

Wait. "Why are they missing it?" I ask.

"Didn't you hear?" Maxine walks over with Ollie, Jocelyn, and Kayla. "I told Rapunzel how mean Tessa and Raza were to AG in the RLW meeting, and she banned them from the party and gave them detention instead." She looks proud of herself, and she should be.

"Wow, I had no idea my sister could be so mean," Jax marvels.

"Rapunzel is your sister?" Jack does a double take.

We're interrupted by the sound of trumpets and violins, which begin to play as Beauty and Prince Sebastian arrive at the party. Beauty and AG are wearing gorgeous blue gowns, and the prince is in a navy dress jacket with gold buttons. Headmistress Flora follows them.

Jack pulls me aside. "Have you seen my mirror anywhere? The last time I saw it, that duck had it."

I pull it out of a handy pocket I sewed into the crinoline under my uniform. "Peaches had it again. You didn't tell me it was magical."

Jack's eyes widen. "You got it to work for you?"

"Yes, and it showed me Anna. You were right," I whisper. A Tom Thumb Catering cart wheels by us. "She looks so sad. I think she wants to leave, and he won't let her."

I notice Jax watching us and stop talking. I don't want to fight with him again.

Jack nods. "Like Mum. We have to save them." He takes my hand. "Listen, I think I have an idea of where they might be." He hesitates. "I saw something in the mirror the other day—my mum being made to work in Cloud City."

Angelina had mentioned the harp was in Cloud City. "What makes you think they're there?"

Jack looks at me strangely. "It's where I went when I climbed the beanstalk last time. Remember?"

"Oh right." I hear a rumble in the distance. Maybe thunder? Strange, the sky is a clear blue.

He scratches his chin. "We just have to find a way up there."

Another rumble of thunder makes the actual ground shake. A few Pegasi bust out of their barn and take flight. A flock of birds zooms by overhead.

"Wow, that's some storm brewing!" Maxine says.

Ollie sniffs the air, licks his finger, and puts it up into the wind. "Funny, but I don't smell a weather change."

"If it's not thunder, then what is that sound, pirate?" Jocelyn asks.

"Gilly!" AG comes running out of the tent toward me, her face flushed with excitement. "Are you coming in? Mother said I could invite my friends to sit at our table. There's room for all of you," she tells the others. "It sounds like it's going to rain. Good thing we have the tent."

Another rumble sends Jax, Maxine, and I colliding into one another. It's quickly followed by a wave of earth-shaking sounds, each one making the ground move more than the time before. Something is definitely not right here.

The ground begins to crack, a line zigzagging from the lake to the castle.

"Earthquake!" AG cries as she and Jack reach for each other to keep from falling.

Kids are screaming as we run to get out of the way. Royals and commoners alike are streaming out of the tent as ogres trip over chairs to get away. We dive for cover behind a stone wall near the school, and I watch in horror as a large green weed begins to grow out of the crack at an alarming speed. It's not an earthquake. It's a beanstalk!

I've never seen an actual beanstalk before. Sure, I've read about them in *Happily Ever After Scrolls* and heard tall tales from kids who swear they've seen one, but nothing could have prepared me for the monstrous plant growing before my eyes. Dozens of electric-green roots burst through the ground near the party tent and quickly wind together into something that looks like a giant tree trunk, stretching and weaving as they grow taller and taller. Smaller branches and leaves burst from the stalks, pushing their branches sideways and breaking whatever is in their path.

"The giants are coming! The giants are coming!" a girl shouts as she runs by us frantically.

I look up, but with the low pink clouds, I can't see the top of the stalk. Maybe it's just a beanstalk. Not every stalk leads to giants, do they?

The Dwarf Police Squad is already directing people away from the stalk as the branches begin to twist and grow around the tent. Rapunzel and Snow are guiding students to safety while Wolfington, Harlow, and Flora start to shoot commands at the stalk to keep it from growing. Their spells don't seem to be working. *Snap!* A thorn on one branch punctures a tent wall, causing the left side to come crashing down.

"We have to do something," says Maxine.

"Look! My parents! They're okay!" AG points to Beauty and Prince Sebastian hurrying a group of fairies out of the way of a falling branch. I can hear Prince Sebastian calling AG's name. She stands up to run to them, but Jack holds out a hand to block us all from leaving.

"Wait!" says Jack.

"Why would we wait?" Jax demands. "People need help, and AG's parents are looking for her."

"Wait!" Jack watches the stalk closely. "You'll get trampled."

"Trampled?" I ask worriedly.

ROARRRRRRRRR!

I know that roar. I've heard it before.

ROARRRRRRRRR!

"It's a giant!" Maxine cries as two giants start descending the beanstalk, which now reaches all the way into the sky.

Jack grabs my hand. "We have to go! This is our chance—the beanstalk will lead us straight to Cloud City!"

His voice is washed away by the sound of a giant stepping onto the ground, making things shake further. Seconds later, the school's extra-loud new warning siren goes off. It whirs as Miri's mirrors on the great lawn flash a deep ruby red. "Fairy Tale Reform School is under attack!" Miri announces. "I repeat, Fairy Tale Reform School is under attack! Defend your school!"

A second giant is right behind the first one. The two stumble around the grounds aimlessly, looking sort of stressed by all the little people taking aim at them. I'm slightly in awe of the sight of them. As tall as a castle turret, with feet as large as Blackbeard's ship, these giants look different from the ones I encountered in the Hollow Woods. Their teeth aren't all yellow, and if I'm not mistaken, one is wearing a rather civilized dress shirt and vest. I see something fly through the air toward us.

"Duck!" I cry as a trident narrowly misses taking off AG's head. I watch her face twist angrily as a hair sprouts from her chin. She quickly calms her breathing, and the hair disappears.

I can see now that mermaids are aiming their tridents and spears at the giants with little success. Their weapons keep bouncing off them and onto the ground. Madame Cleo, posed on a rock with fiery-red hair, uses her magic mirror to conjure a whirlpool that whips at such a frantic speed I worry the rest of the mermaids will be washed away. Instead, the first giant gets caught up in the tidal wave and starts to fall. Everyone cheers, but the victory is short lived. The giant stumbles backward and falls into the Pegasus barn.

My throat constricts. Where is Maximus? Is he okay? I look up and breathe a sigh of relief. He's already in midflight. The sky is full of Pegasi and flying carpets, which hopefully means none were still in the now-crushed barn.

"Those clumsy giants could destroy the school with one wrong move," Jocelyn shouts as the second giant trips and squashes the vegetable garden with one footstep. "Is anyone still inside the school?"

"Peaches, Wilson, and the fairy pets are," Maxine realizes at the same time I do.

"And Tessa and Raza are in the dungeon. Right, Jack?" Jax says. "Jack?" We turn to look for him, but he's gone.

ROARRRRRRRR! The giants are now pointing at the castle.

My eyes move from where Jack was just standing to the beanstalk and back to the school.

Anna.

Wilson. Peaches.

Anna.

The RLWs I can't stand.

Anna.

I feel pulled in two completely different directions. I look at my home-away-from-home one more time. We can't hope the giants are stopped before they get to the castle walls. We have to get everyone out in case they do.

Jax is watching me, waiting for me to say the right thing. This time I do.

"We have to go inside and get everyone out." I whistle for Maximus, and like magic, the Pegasus lands at my feet. Jax climbs on behind me. "But first we need to make a stop at my dorm room. I think I'm going to need my bow and arrow."

CHAPTER 13

Under Attack

There's no time to waste. I call out orders from atop Maximus. "Kayla, Jocelyn, and Ollie, make sure Kayla's mom is secure," I direct them as they jump onto other Pegasi and join us in flight while Maxine takes off on Blue. "Maxine and AG, you release the fairy pets. Jax and I will grab Peaches and Wilson. Then, we'll get Tessa and Raza out. We will meet back out here at this wall, or what's left of it, when we're done. Got it?"

"Got it!" everyone agrees.

I look at AG. I've added her to our crew without even asking. Knowing how she handles stress, is this a good idea? "We can get you back to your parents if you want." I say.

AG stares at the sky filled with cannon smoke, wand flares, and Pegasi. "No," she says firmly. "I want to help."

I look at her.

"I can handle this."

I nod.

"Any clue where Jack went?" Ollie asks me.

I stare at the beanstalk again and wonder whether Jack has left me behind to try to rescue his family. I hear a piercing scream and look down. One of the giants has just crushed what remained of the welcome tea tent. I can't think about that right now.

"No clue! Everyone, let's go!" I watch until they make it past the giants, then turn my focus back to Maximus.

"Hey, boy." I know he can understand me. "Dorms, then the dungeon. In that order."

Maximus's wings flap fast to get us above the giants, the school, and the destruction. You can see everything from up here. Magic carpets whiz over and under giants' noses and through their legs as kids riding Pegasi throw anything they can find to slow the giants down. We're high enough now that I can see my teachers, as tiny as ants, still trying to blast the beanstalk, which continues to shimmer and glow and grow.

I urge Maximus to go faster, leading him straight toward the roof of the girls' dormitories. We set down on the smoky roof, and Jax and I dismount. A fire is blazing in the woods in the distance. "I'm going to send Peaches and Wilson up to you," I tell Maximus. "Fly them to Kayla's mom's fairy hut, then come back for us here. We're going to get the others out of the dungeon. Then we'll return to the roof." I hesitate. "But take off again if it gets dangerous."

I will wait for you, Maximus somehow tells me.

THUMP. THUMP. The giants' movements seem to be getting closer.

"We don't have much time," Jax says as we descend the stairs from the roof toward my dorm room. "The giants could slam a fist through one of these walls at any moment."

Rushing down the winding steps, we make it to my dorm room quickly. Peaches and Wilson start honking and squeaking the minute they see me.

"Guys, we need to get you out of here," I tell them. "Jax will carry you up to Maximus, and he'll get you to safety."

For the first time ever, Peaches doesn't try to nip me. Wilson nuzzles my fingers, then hops onto Peaches's back. Jax holds open a sack and places the pair inside so that Maximus can hold the bag in his teeth. As Jax carries the pair up to the roof, I feel a slight wave of relief.

I run back to my room and grab my bow and arrow. Now I'm ready for action.

Finding our way into the dungeon is the harder part of the mission. With the warning sirens going off and all the explosions outside school, the hallways are going haywire. The destruction sounds far away inside the cool, darkened castle, but the trembles continue. Hallways glitch open and shut at lightning speed, making it tricky to get through them. Suddenly, I hear yelling.

"Girls in pink sashes being held against their will! *Help!*"

Awesome sauce! We've found the dungeons! A rumbling crash from somewhere inside the castle makes us move faster. My hand is on my bow and arrow as I run down the steps and find Tessa and Raza crying and clinging to the bars. I can't believe they're really behind bars!

"Madame Cleo let Blackbeard take over detention, and this is where he placed us," Tessa sobs. "Now rescue me." She sees Jax and stops crying. "On second thought, let Prince Jaxon." I roll my eyes.

Jax grabs the keys from the wall and starts unlocking the

cell doors while I keep watch. The ground rumbles, and tiny pieces of cement rain down on our heads. Tessa and Raza run out of the cell and collapse tearfully into Jax's arms.

"It was terrible! We've been locked in there for an hour, and no one came to get us out!" Raza cries.

"That's because the school is under attack by giants, and a huge beanstalk just sprouted on the grounds," I tell them. I glance around the dungeon. This place always spooks me—too many things have gone wrong down here. It doesn't help that Alva's statue is down here now too.

"Giants? A beanstalk?" Tessa gasps. "I thought it was a thunderstorm!"

"We need to get out of here," Raza adds, clinging to Jax's arm tightly. "I can't have my last moments be in a dungeon!"

I'm about to lead the way back to the roof when the hallway disappears. Before I can find a new way out, the room begins to shake and debris begins flying in our direction. Both girls scream. Jax grabs them and pulls them into a doorway. I join them just as the wall to the next chamber comes crumbling down as if it's been blasted to smithereens. The gaping hole gives me a clear view of Alva's statue, as a meaty arm pounds its way through what remains of the ceiling, narrowly missing her.

"A giant!" Raza shouts.

I smack my hand over her mouth, but my arm is visibly shaking as I try to keep her quiet. The giant may come after us if it knows we're here, but my fear is short lived. Seconds later, I watch in horror as Princess Rose's former captor is lifted off her stone podium, clenched in the grip of the giant's hand.

I know immediately who sent these giants. There's only one person who needs Alva to complete his spell. She may still be stone, but I can't let her fall into Rumpelstiltskin's hands. I have an arrow out of my quiver before I even realize it. I take aim at the giant's fingers and fire again and again. I see the giant's grip on the statue loosen slightly, then tighten again as it lifts Alva through the crater of a ceiling.

"No!" I run from the doorway as the ceiling continues to give way.

"Gilly!" Jax shouts, but I keep running till I reach the giant's hand and Alva's statue. I jump for the statue's pointy shoes, my fingers grazing the soles as the giant lifts the statue completely out of reach and it is carried into the darkened sky.

I scream out in frustration.

Maximus must hear me because seconds later he's landing in the remains of the dungeon.

I calmly turn to my best friend. "Jax, you have to listen to me. Stiltskin is up in Cloud City. I saw Anna there in Jack's mirror, and he saw his mum there too. I know you don't trust him, but this isn't just about trying to get to Anna anymore. I would bet my bow and arrow that Stiltskin sent that giant to retrieve Alva for him, and Grimm only knows how long it will take him to bring her back to life again. Then it's game over for Enchantasia."

Jax balls his hands into fists. "Gilly, Stiltskin is expecting you to follow him! He knows how worried you must be about Anna and how badly you want her to come home. I told you before: he could be leading you into a trap."

I don't have time to come up with a fancy argument. Instead, I go with the truth. "She's my sister, and it's my fault she's with Rump. I have to try to get to her. I know she's still good! I just know it! Even if she's not, if there's the slightest chance that she's in danger, I *have* to try to help her. If I don't, I'll never forgive myself."

Jax groans in frustration as Maximus paws at the rubble. "Fine. But we're going with you."

"You are?" I say with a mixture of relief and hope.

I stare at Jax's face covered with ash and his dress uniform torn and tattered. He seems to struggle to find the words. "I may not trust Jack, but I trust you. We have to try to stop Stiltskin from getting Alva. *If* Anna wants to come home, I'll do my best to help make that happen too."

I grab Jax tight and don't let go. He holds me just as tight.

Tessa's voice cuts through the darkness. "Are we getting out of this dungeon or what?"

Jax and I quickly pull apart, helping Tessa and Raza on Maximus before we take off in flight. Maximus flies quickly through the smoky sky to what's left of the wall we left just a short time ago. In the distance, I can see the giants already climbing back up the beanstalk with their Alva statue. The FTRS grounds are a mess of flattened rubble. When Maximus lands, Tessa and Raza run off to find more RLWs. But Jocelyn, Maxine, Ollie, Kayla, and AG are waiting by the wall, safe and sound, and Blue is hovering nearby. Maxine pulls us in for a group hug.

"When we saw the giants with the statue, we thought the worst!" Maxine sniffs, practically suffocating me with her right arm. "Are Peaches and Wilson okay? Kayla's mom is fine. Blackbeard's ship caught fire from a training wand misfire, and the professors are helping put it out. We should go help them and then figure out how to get that statue back."

I pull out of the hug. "I already have a plan." The others look at me. "We're going up the beanstalk after Alva's statue. Hopefully we can bring Anna and any other squad members who have changed their minds about working with Stiltskin home too. But first we have to get up the beanstalk and find our way to Cloud City. I think that's where Stiltskin's hiding." I quickly explain what Kayla and I saw in Jack's mirror and what Jack told me before. The others don't fight me.

"If we're going up there, Jack should lead us," Jocelyn says. "He's been there before. I'm sure there is more than one giant city in the clouds. We need to make sure we find the right one. Has anyone seen him?"

"Not since before the battle," Ollie points out.

AG points to the shimmering beanstalk and its tangle of vines. "Is that him over there?" It's hard to see through all the smoke, but I can make out a boy who looks like Jack and is about to climb a beanstalk.

"I think so," I say.

Jax whistles for Blue. "Let's go!" Ollie and AG climb on with him, while Jocelyn and I take Maximus with Maxine.

Kayla flies alongside us at warp speed. Maximus and Blue land before the tangle of vines, right next to where Jack is surveying the beanstalk.

Jack turns toward us. "Gilly! Where have you been? I looked everywhere for you."

"You did?" Jax is skeptical. "Funny, you seemed to disappear when things got hairy."

"I had to go get these." Jack holds up a small, shiny knife. "Coal miner daggers. The only dagger tough enough to stick to a beanstalk vine and help you climb it. I brought one for you. Are you coming? We have to get up there before Stiltskin cuts down the stalk so no one can follow."

I didn't even think of that problem. He hands me a dagger, and I stake it easily into the vine, making my first foothold. Jax puts out a hand to stop Jack from doing the same.

"We're coming with you too," Jax tells him.

"No way," Jack says. "This is a dangerous mission! Do you want to become giant stew? I can help one person hide out in Cloud City from those nasty giants. Not a whole crew."

"You're going to have to," Kayla says. "Gilly helped me get my family back, and now I'm going to help her get hers. And, you know, save Enchantasia too."

"We're a team," Ollie adds, "and teams stick together."

The others agree.

"Do you know where the harp is?" Maxine asks.

"Where Stiltskin's camping out?" Jocelyn wonders.

"Are you sure you can even find your way back to the city?" Jax adds.

"Relax," Jack tells us. "I've found the harp before. I can find it again."

"Gilly, are you *sure* this is a good idea?" Maxine whispers to me. "How do you know we can trust Jack? We barely know him. What if he leaves us up there?"

"We'll be okay if we're together," I promise Maxine.

"What about me? Am I part of the team too?" AG asks. "Because I really want to come. I have my own reasons for wanting to find Stiltskin."

"Of course you are," I say and look at Jack. "I hope you have more daggers. If you want my help getting your mum and cow back, these guys are coming too."

"The fire's out on the ship." Jocelyn notices. "The professors will notice us soon. We should move."

Jack bangs his head against the stalk vine in frustration. "Fine! There are more daggers in my pack. I always have extras in case I lose one." He begrudgingly offers us each a silver blade.

"Funny how you brought them to Fairy Tale Reform School not knowing a beanstalk would ever sprout," Jax says as he looks at the blade in his hand.

"Think what you want, Prince." Jack gives me a look. "I am always prepared. You should thank me."

I stake the dagger in the vine again and pull myself up higher. "He'll thank you once we reach the top. Right now, it's time to climb."

CHAPTER 14

Cloud City

W e are so high up.

I look down and immediately wish I hadn't. Next, I look up, and I'm not sure what's worse. My friends are climbing above me, Kayla and Ollie so far ahead that their bodies are covered by the clouds. Blue sky surrounds me as far as the eye can see. Once in a while, a cloud floats by, veiling the stalk from sight. It's scary when that happens, but Jack says we can't stop moving. Stiltskin could cut the stalk down at any moment, and if he doesn't, our professors could do the same from below. *Ouch!* One of the thorns on the vine pricks my wrist, and it starts to bleed.

Jack made climbing a beanstalk seem so easy.

"Just a few more feet!" he calls from above.

With the last of my strength, I stake the dagger into the next piece of vine and pull myself up. I step gingerly onto a cloud, holding my breath to see if I fall right through. I don't. It feels squishy and has a bit of a bounce to it, but it holds my weight. I'm not sure what I'm expecting to see at the top of the beanstalk, but it's certainly not more clouds, birds, and blue sky. I don't see any sign of a city.

"There's nothing here, bean brain!" Jocelyn snaps at Jack. "You've brought us on a wild-goose chase up the wrong beanstalk. This one must have been a decoy!"

"What are we going to do?" Maxine asks.

AG covers her face with her nicked hands. Everyone but Jack has gotten cut on the climb up. "I'm too tired to climb down again, and I don't want to face my father." She looks like she might start sobbing, which will bring out her hairy side.

I shake her. "Deep breaths. In. Out." AG practices her breathing. "Better?" She nods.

"Everyone done freaking out?" Jack asks. "Because the city is right in front of you."

I squint harder. "I don't see anything."

"Me neither," says Jax.

Jack sighs. "Giants may be dumb and mean, but they aren't clueless. You think they want people using magic beans to climb up here and steal their fortunes? No way! After I came up the first time, they put some protection charms up. Look harder."

He slices his hand through a cloud in front of us. For a split second, I see a shimmering city in the distance. The buildings are as tan as sand and look exactly like the ones I saw in the mirror. That must be where Anna is.

"Let's go," I say, anxious to get there.

Jack stops us. "If you want to survive, I'm in charge up here." He looks at Jax. "Don't listen, and you'll be a giant's lunch in seconds."

Eaten by a giant? Not the way I want to go. "What do we need to do?" I ask.

"And how do we know you won't lead us into a giant's rotten mouth?" Jax asks.

"Giants can smell you before they can see you," Jack says, looking around. "They'll know we're coming, and so will Stiltskin. If he's here—and I think he is—he'll be in the city center. We have to mask our scent." Jack steps into the cloud again, then back out with a bright-orange flower. "This will do it. They're dragon fire flowers. They grow frequently near the edge of town." He passes them around. "Giants hate the smell of them." He begins rubbing a petal on his arms. "Slather some of this on, and no one will even notice you. Not that you still can't get stepped on by accident," he adds. "And this stuff will only last so long. Of course, even if we succeed, we have to find a way down the stalk without them shaking us off. *If* the stalk is even still there."

"So if they see us, we get eaten. If they smell us, we get eaten. And if we avoid both, we can still get trapped here?" Ollie asks, placing a flower in the pocket of his dirty shirt. "Great odds."

Jax rubs a petal on his forehead. "Let's get in there and find Anna, your family, the squad kids who want to go home, and the harp."

"About the harp…" Jack steps into the cloud and disappears. "It can't be lifted out of here. It's why I couldn't take it with me last time I climbed up. The harp only moves when it's being played, and it can only be played by someone with pure love for another."

"You never mentioned that before," I say as I rub the petal on my neck.

Jack sticks his head back out of the cloud. "I'm sure we'll figure something out. Come on! And be quiet!"

I'm the last one through the cloud. When I come out the other side, I am in awe. If I thought the beanstalk was high, Cloud City's buildings are even higher! They're modeled after the ones we have in Enchantasia, but everything is giant in size, and the whole city is tan. Every building looks like it's floating in midair. There aren't many flowers or decorations though. The city is pretty plain, which is surprising since everything I've ever learned about giants taught me their world was full of riches they had stolen from our kingdoms. We walk quickly past a doorway higher than the roof at FTRS. A cloud floats by, obscuring the home in front of us from view.

We walk in silence for a while, each of us staring up at the buildings in awe. They're so large it could take five minutes to *walk* by just one of them, and at this rate, it's going to take forever to get to the city center even if the streets are deserted. *Where is everyone?*

Suddenly, everyone who is in front of me stops. AG is pointing frantically at a wall. I use a cloud to bounce over to her and see the red, childlike lettering on the side of a building.

WARNING! Rump zone! Resisting is futile! Escape we must!

It looks like someone has tried to wash the message off but couldn't. Some of the red paint has dripped down the side of the wall. I look down at the ground and spot a human-sized scrap of scroll blowing in the wind. There's part of a message written on it in scratchy script.

...by the Trickster! Run! Hide! Or you will be imprisoned like the others!

Running? Hiding? Was this written by a giant? Or a squad member who wants to leave and can't?

Jack takes the paper from my hands and reads it himself. "I don't understand," he whispers. "These weren't here the last time. They look like giants' handwriting, but who would those lugheads be afraid of? They can eat people in one bite."

The cloud we're on starts to shake, and we hold on to the building to steady ourselves. I can't see anything through the mist and cloud cover. Jack is motioning wildly, but I don't know what he's saying. Suddenly a large, dirty hand comes into view.

AG freezes in fear, but I pull her along as we press ourselves against the nearest wall. Jack tries to push the door open so we can hide, but it's too heavy to move. We're trapped.

The giant walks out of the nearest cloud right in front of us. Great. We've already given ourselves away. Any second the rest of the giants will come running. My mouth feels dry, and my hands are clammy. I place my hand in front of AG to protect her, but then I notice something different about this giant. It's much shorter, and its face looks so young.

Is it a baby giant?

Jack pulls his dagger back out of his pack and prepares to aim it at the giant's arm.

"Wait!" I shout. "I think it's a toddler!"

The giant opens its mouth and smiles, revealing a single tooth. Then its left hand comes through the cloud, and I see it's holding a bottle! The giant sees Maxine, who is the largest of our group, and giggles. The sound is so loud that we have to hold our ears, but I'm relieved. It's just a baby!

But then a larger arm comes into view, swooping the baby high into the air. The toddler drops his bottle, which crushes the corner of a fence just feet from where we're standing. AG screams. If no one knew we were here before, they definitely know we're here now. AG's hands start to grow fur at an alarming rate, and I know it's any second before she howls and gives our location away. The momma giant looks at AG and roars. I clutch my bow and arrow, ready to fight her off before she can snatch us and make us a toddler snack.

"Run!" Jack shouts. "Run!"

Before any of us can move, the giant takes off with her baby, running in the opposite direction. She glances back at us as she runs, and I could swear she actually looks frightened. What the fairy is going on?

"Guys, I think that giant was afraid of us," Jax says.

"Don't be a fool, Prince." Jack rolls his eyes. "Giants eat people and crush villages. They're not scared of humans. They hate us. I've seen it with my own eyes."

"Maybe they were just mad at you because you stole from them," Maxine guesses. We all look at Jack, who opens his mouth to speak and says nothing.

"Or maybe they think humans hate them." Jocelyn motions to the piece of scroll in her hand. "Both this flyer and that sign on the wall make me think they're trying to escape our kind."

"Or if not our kind, then Rumpelstiltskin," Ollie says.

I've never seen Jack look so doubtful. He pulls the scroll from Jocelyn's hands. "But...you saw the giants at FTRS. They were attacking us."

"Did anyone else think they looked kind of confused?" Kayla asks.

"Yeah, they kept stumbling around as if they didn't know where to go, until they headed for Alva's statue. Once they got it, they left," Jax adds.

"How did Stiltskin know where the statue was hidden anyway?" Maxine asks.

In the distance, we hear a roar. My hand goes to my bow and arrow again. The others touch the coal miner daggers strapped to their waists.

"Either way, we should probably stay on high alert," says Ollie. "You know, just in case."

AG looks positively green.

ROAR!

There it is again. We look around, but the streets are still deserted. Jack runs ahead of us. When he reaches the next block—which takes him a while since we're so small compared to giant dwellings—he stops short and stares at something we can't see. With the threat obviously low, we all follow, bouncing on the clouds to get there faster.

ROAR!

When we reach Jack, I see why he's stopped. It's another

giant, but this scene is different from the one before. My stomach clenches. This giant is being pushed around by a bunch of kids. Kids wearing familiar gold crests on their gold shirts. It's the Stiltskin Squad.

I immediately step forward to look for Anna, but Jax holds me back. We huddle behind a giant garbage can, which smells like dead fish. I watch the kids bark orders.

"I said *move*! You didn't do your job, and now you're punished!" one kid yells at the giant.

"Don't you get what we're saying, you big oaf?" another girl barks, and I wince.

I recognize that voice. It's Gretel! My eyes narrow sharply as I hone in on the evil candy thief who corrupted my baby sister.

Hansel walks up behind her. "You were supposed to be forcing other giants to go down the beanstalk, and instead you let them escape!" He steals the giant's food, and it roars so loudly that Kayla falls over. We pick her up and pull her behind the garbage can again. "We could have flattened that stupid school, but now thanks to you, we're down more giant slaves. Where are they hiding?" The giant just blinks. "Tell us!"

Maxine starts to tear up. It's awful to watch them bullying this poor giant. I look at Jack. His face is pale. I don't think he had any clue the giants were being abused.

"Now we have to worry about that moronic hero and her friends coming up here to stop us!" Hansel yells at the giant. "No food for you today!" The giant's face looks so sad. "You get back to that beanstalk and climb down it to keep those kids from climbing up, or your friends won't eat either. You hear? And bring some others with you or you'll be punished for that too."

"Stop hurting him!"

A girl runs over to the giant and touches his arm tenderly. My heart catches in my throat.

It's Anna.

CHAPTER 15

The Rescue Mission

M y eyes fill with tears at the sight of my little sister. Anna doesn't look like she's in danger, but she does look pretty dirty. Her prized brown hair, which was always combed neatly and held with a clip, is stringy and frizzy. There are dark rings under her eyes like she hasn't slept in weeks. It gives me hope that maybe my hunch was right. Anna isn't happy here anymore. Maybe she's actually learned her lesson.

The giant bursts into tears.

"Stop crying," Hansel yells at him. "Just get the job done so we can get out of the sky already. I'm so ready to go home."

"We're not going home, remember?" Gretel tells him.

"Stiltskin is going to create a new Enchantasia for us." She glares at the giant. "As long as you people don't mess it up."

"*You people?*" Maxine forms a fist. "Who does she think she is?"

"Anna," Hansel demands. "Get this giant to do his job. Stiltskin wants FTRS destroyed so there are no more complications. Got it?"

Anna hesitates. "I think so."

Gretel grabs Anna by the collar and glares at her. "You're not going to let another giant go, are you? He's not going to go easy on you a second time."

"I know." Anna's voice is shaky. "I won't screw up again."

"Don't disappoint him." Gretel walks away, leaving Anna alone with the giant, who is still crying. Soon Anna is too.

Before anyone can stop me, I'm bouncing onto the nearest cloud and calling Anna's name. "Anna!" I shout, running toward her.

Anna wipes her eyes as if she can't believe what she's seeing. Then her face breaks into a smile. "Gilly?" She runs toward me.

When we reach each other, we hang on to each other, both dissolving in tears. I'm not sure what makes me happier—that I found her, or that she seems happy to see me. I don't ever want to let her go again.

"How did you find me? How did you even get up here?" Anna clings to me. "I thought I'd never see you again! I was afraid I'd be stuck here forever."

My words come out rushed, tumbling over one another as I say all the things I should have when she was at FTRS. "I never stopped looking for you. I'm so sorry, Anna. I'm so sorry that I didn't see how much you were hurting about Father and the shop. It's my fault you're here now—I pushed you toward him!"

"No, it's not your fault," Anna insists, her eyes brimming with tears. "He made me so many promises, and I was foolish to believe him. By the time I realized the truth, it was too late to get away." Her face is full of anguish. "I'd already made a deal with him."

"That deal is broken," I say feverishly, even though I have no clue if I can do that. "You're coming home with me...that is, if you want to." My voice catches in my throat.

She starts to laugh through her tears. "Of course I want to!" The two of us are still crying and hugging when Jocelyn pokes me in the shoulder.

"Sorry to break up the happy reunion, but we've got to get going." Jocelyn looks closely at Anna. "You'd better be worth this rescue."

"Jocelyn!" I reprimand her.

"It's true!" Jocelyn scoffs. "Did you ask her where the harp is?"

Jack steps forward. "Or my mum or cow?" He holds out his hand to Anna. 'I'm Jack. You might have heard of me. I was the first kid to climb a beanstalk and reach Cloud City."

Anna interrupts him. "Did you say harp? Stiltskin has it at his headquarters up here." The others walk over, but there is no time for reunions or introductions. "He's planning to use it so he can—"

"Rewind time, take over the kingdom, doom us all. We already know all that." Jax is hasty. "What we need to do now is stop him."

"And rescue other kids like you who want to leave his squad," Maxine adds.

"There are some," Anna tells us. "Jack's mum might be there too. Those of us who don't do as we're told usually wind up in the dungeon, which is at the headquarters." Her lip quivers. "I'm on my last warning."

"Then we need to move fast and get you, those kids, and the harp out of here," I say. "What else do you know?"

"He needs more ingredients for his spell, but he's frustrated because they're in some book and we haven't found it yet," Anna explains. A look passes between me and Kayla. "He has the harp, but it is tricky to control. It can't be moved unless it's playing, and it won't play unless it, um, likes the person singing to it."

"Told you," Jack sings. "Or I said something like that. I think."

"Come again?" asks Jax.

Anna's cheeks color. "When the harp is playing music, it's said to be as light as a feather. When it's not, it weighs more than a thousand giants. It's why no man has been able to steal it."

"Nothing can weigh that much," Ollie says. "*Can* it?"

"The harp does," Jack says. "I should know. I tried to steal it once but couldn't get it to play." He scratches his chin. "Guess my intentions weren't exactly on the up-and-up."

"You probably wanted to sell it to buy more cows," Jax grumbles.

"There's only one cow for me," Jack tells him. "Besides, I wasn't sure how I'd get that thing down the beanstalk."

"Rumpelstiltskin has tried everything to trick the harp into playing—making deals, casting spells, offering sacrifices. He keeps making people sing to the harp, but they all wind up getting zapped. The harp doesn't like to be tricked." Anna shows off a scar on her right arm. "I know it sounds silly, but the harp will only play for someone completely pure of heart. Someone who wants to use its music for good. I guess he thought the harp would play if he was able to save Alva, since they were together a long time ago, but he hasn't figured out how to reverse her curse."

"Maybe you and your sister can sing to it," Jack suggests, and we all look at him. "Okay, so maybe your sister is a Stiltskin Squad member so she isn't one hundred percent pure, but you are." He looks at me. "You're here to rescue her, and you want to save the harp, not sell it. The harp will sense that."

"That might be the first thing you've said that makes sense," Jocelyn agrees.

"It's still risky," Maxine worries. "What if Gilly gets hurt?"

"I'm with Jack." Anna grasps my hands. "I think you can make it happen. Then we can all go home."

Home. I can almost see Anna sitting in our boot, around

the table with Mother and Father, Han, Hamish, Trixie, Felix, and me home on break (for getting an A on Prince Sebastian's family tree paper). I want that to happen so badly I can taste it. "Okay. I'll give it a shot."

"I don't know…" Jax hesitates. "My gut is telling me things could go really wrong."

Anna bares her teeth. One of her teeth gleams gold like Stiltskin's. I wonder if she's had so much candy with him that she's had to get a tooth replaced. "You have a better idea, royal?"

Jax raises his right eyebrow.

"Anna," I say in surprise. "Don't talk to Jax that way. He's my friend."

"Sorry." Anna holds her head. "I don't know what's come over me. I have these outbursts… I guess I've been around him too long." She grabs my shoulders. "You have to get me out of here."

I hold her tight. "I will, but first we need to rescue the others and steal the harp."

"And figure out how to get back down the beanstalk," Jocelyn says. "Once he knows we're here, it's going to be tough."

"A magic bean would do the trick," Anna says. "They're useful for getting out of sticky situations. If you have a bean, you just throw it down and it will grow or expand on the spot, taking you wherever you ask it to go." Her eyes widen. "Did you know stalks can grow up, down, sideways, or even open doors to other lands? The places I've seen…" I hate that she still sounds somewhat fascinated by Stiltskin.

ROAR! WAAH!

The giant next to us startles everyone by bursting into tears again. I almost forgot he was there.

"Erp, these are my friends. They won't hurt you." She looks at me. "And this is my sister." She smiles. "I can take you guys to headquarters. Alva's statue was brought there too. He's usually holed up in there spinning gold, but he should be gone right now. He likes to take dinner on a cloud overlooking Enchantasia's royal court castles. He likes to tell the squad stories of what he'll do once the kingdom is his to rule."

I shudder at the thought.

Anna looks at a giant clock on the city wall, then unties Erp, who continues to sniffle. "We should hurry though." She snaps her fingers at Erp. "Take us to Rumpelstiltskin's castle." Erp doesn't move. "*Erp*," Anna says sternly, her voice and face becoming hard. "*Now*."

"Geez, talk about a one-eighty," I hear Jocelyn say. I give her a look.

Erp starts quaking. The Stiltskin Squad must have really done a number on him.

Anna stomps her foot on his palm. "Erp, I'm warning you!"

"Hey," I say softly. "It might work better if you're nice to him." I stare into Erp's big, brown eyes. "If you help get us to headquarters, we will let you go. Then you can try to escape."

Erp slowly lowers his hand so we can all jump in.

"Thanks, Erp." I feel pleased and look at Anna. Her frown is quickly replaced by a tight smile.

"You've saved the day again," she says quietly.

Now I feel bad. AG is looking at us. I don't want Anna to always feel like she's in my shadow. "Not true," I start to say. "You're the one who helped Erp in the first place." Anna doesn't look convinced.

"You're so lucky to have each other," AG blurts out as Erp starts to move.

Anna seems to notice her for the first time. "And you are?"

AG blushes. "Beauty and Prince Sebastian's daughter." I

watch Anna's face dawn with recognition. "Gilly has helped me so much since I've gotten to school."

"That's so nice for you," Anna says, and I can detect a hint of bitterness.

I pull Anna closer. "We're going to get out of here together, and things will be different when you're back. You'll see." Anna manages a small smile.

In the palm of Erp's callused hand, it feels like we're barely moving, but clouds and buildings fly by. I squint my eyes at the bright light growing closer in the distance. As it comes into view, I realize it's a human-sized building washed in a gold color. Stiltskin's headquarters. The jeweled *R* on the center of the door lets everyone know whose place this is. The sun bounces off the gold on the building, making it impossible to look at it straight on without sunglasses. It's strange to see something so tiny in the middle of a giant city.

AG frowns. "This place is kind of elaborate for temporary housing." Erp places us gently on the ground.

"Says the girl with the pop-up castle," Jocelyn quips.

"Stiltskin had the giants build him these headquarters when we came up here," Anna explains. "He's been ostracized in every kingdom we've visited, so we finally put down roots in the clouds. He hated how big everything was when he was so, um, small in stature so he had them build this beautiful castle. He says it will do for now." Anna steps off Erp's hand and walks to the front door, which is, surprisingly, silver. She presses her hand to a lock. It opens. "Follow me."

Jax hangs back to talk to me. So does Jocelyn. "Your sister still seems sort of fascinated with him, don't you think?" His eyes search mine. "And the way she spoke to that giant…"

"You heard her," I say. "She's been with Rump too long. His attitude is rubbing off on her. When I get her home, she'll be fine." *I hope.*

"It's kind of convenient that everyone is at dinner and the harp is unguarded right now." Jocelyn lips are pulled tight. "We should watch our backs." I quiet the uncomfortable feeling in my stomach.

"Come on," Anna calls to us. "The harp is upstairs."

I hurry after her, walking through a very messy dining room. Maps wallpaper the walls, crisscrossed with red strings linking one kingdom to the next. Papers and books cover the table, and crumpled pieces of parchment litter the floor.

Jocelyn makes wild hand motions toward the dining

room mantel, where a jar is glowing iridescent green. "*Beans*," she mouths. "Those are the beans Anna was talking about!"

Jax and I look toward the mantel. I remember seeing a jar like that at Fairy Tale Reform School when Stiltskin was in charge.

"That's our ticket home," Jax whispers. "You heard Anna. Those beans can open doorways and lead us anywhere we want to go."

"What are you guys doing?" Anna startles us. "We only have fifteen minutes!"

"I spotted a map of Fairy Tale Reform School." Jocelyn points to the blueprints on the back wall. I didn't even notice it. "I wanted to see what he wrote on it. If he's going to attack again, we should know what he's after."

Anna walks past the beans, and I inhale sharply. Her hand rests on the map. "That's a map of everywhere we've looked for his villain origin story. His gut tells him the book is at Fairy Tale Reform School, but so far we've turned up nothing."

We?

Anna grabs my hand—she hasn't done that since we were little—and smiles tentatively. "Now we really must move. We have a trickster to stop."

CHAPTER 16

Music of My Heart

Stiltskin's house is bigger than it looks from the outside. We move past dorm-style bedrooms with bunk beds, common rooms filled with jars of candy, and even a second kitchen. Pots and pans crowd the sink, and flour covers the table. Finally, the house opens up to an atrium with a dome-like glass ceiling. In the center is Alva's statue. And it's sitting next to the golden harp. The wood looks strong yet weathered, as if it's been around for a long time, and flecks of gold shine on the strings. A shadow crosses the atrium glass, and I look up. One of Erp's giant-sized eyes is watching us through the glass.

"Go away!" Anna shoos him. "You're going to give us away!" Erp's eye moves out of view. "There are too many people in this room! Someone is going to trigger an alarm."

"While you guys try to get the harp to play, we'll go to the dungeon and try to rescue the others," Ollie suggests. "We'll meet back here. Okay?"

"Yes." Anna looks relieved. "I don't have a key to the cells, but there must be one down there somewhere. You guys are good at picking locks, aren't you?"

Ollie salutes her. "I'm on it, Captain. Who wants to help?"

"My mum and cow are down there," Jack says. "I'm definitely going."

Kayla and Maxine volunteer too. Jocelyn decides to keep watch at the door with AG. Jax walks over to the harp and attempts to strum the strings. There's no sound, but it doesn't try to zap him at least. He's not evil.

"See what I mean?" Anna tsks. "It won't even play for a *royal*."

Since when does Anna say *royal* like it's a bad word?

I step around the harp, looking at it from all angles.

"Are you ready to sing?" Anna asks hopefully. "I know the harp will play for you. It knows how hard you've fought to find me and how true your love is." Her eyes are like saucers, and I worry she's going to cry again. "You've always looked out for me."

"You really mean that?" I ask. As a hard lump develops in my throat, I realize just how badly I needed to hear her say those words. She really does know how sorry I am for pushing her away. I love her so much and just want her to be happy. That's what I've always wanted, even if I never said it till now.

"Of course," Anna says. "You've always been there for me. Now it's my turn to be there for you." She gives my hand another squeeze, and I beam. "Sing something."

I try to think of a song from my heart, a song that means something to both of us. "What about Father's lullaby? The one he always sang at bedtime."

"Yes! The one he sang on the evenings he was actually done making shoes in time to see us off to bed?" Anna says. "Do you still remember the words?"

"How could I forget them?" I ask.

"Be ready, guys!" Jocelyn says, running back over. "If this works, everyone is going to need to pitch in to carry this thing," Jax, AG, and Jocelyn gather around the harp.

"I'm sure the harp can be heard all over the city," Jax adds. "He'll know we're here and send everyone after us. We'll have to get to the beanstalk fast."

"I've brought a few extra hands." Ollie, Kayla, and Maxine are back, and they've got a group of twenty kids who have definitely seen better days. Many of them look familiar. They're still in their FTRS uniforms, but their clothes are tattered and their faces dirty. Porter looks thinner than I remember, and the twins from the village look like they haven't slept in weeks. They all file around the harp. Erp's eye comes back into view. Jack rushes over to me in a panic.

"My mum and cow weren't there," he says. "Where could they be?"

"We'll find them after we do this," I tell Jack. "We won't leave without them."

"Gilly." Jax sounds like he's going to argue.

"We have to help them," I insist even though the stakes are piling high against us. How are we getting all these kids down the stalk and the harp too? "We'll be okay."

Anna takes my hand again. Her brow furrows worriedly, like it would when I'd bring her a present that she knew had been stolen. "I'm scared."

"Don't be." I place one hand on the harp and take a deep breath. I'm not really a singer—and I've certainly never sung in public—but I know the words to this song backward and forward. I look at Anna as I begin to sing:

> *When the sky has gone from day to night,*
> *I tuck my little ones in tight.*
> *Soft and snuggled in your beds,*
> *I hope that warm thoughts fill your heads.*

I don't hear any sound at first. But around the third line, I feel a rush through my bones. My body starts to tingle, starting at my head and spreading quickly to my toes and to my fingers like an electric charge is shooting through my veins. My eyes widen in surprise, and so do Anna's.

"Something is happening!" Maxine cries as the harp strings begin to come to life creating the song's melody. "Keep singing!"

> *I love to sit and watch you dream,*
> *While lacing shoes and sewing seams.*
> *I'd sew one hundred thousand shoes*
> *To make all of your dreams come true.*
> *And if I had to start anew,*
> *I'd do it all again for you.*
> *My children, my heart, my dearest ones,*
> *Sleep well until the night is done.*

The tingly melodic sound is breathtaking. The harp matches me note for note, as if it always knew what I would sing. Even though I know the music means Stiltskin isn't far behind, I feel very calm, like I'm meant to be here right now. Around us, everyone's eyes brighten at the lovely melody. Even Erp is listening. *I'm doing it!*

With Anna by my side, and the harp playing the melody of my heart, I feel happier than I have in months. I hold the final note as long as I can, knowing it's the moment of truth. Everyone closes in on our circle to help move the harp. Jack touches it again, and it easily lifts off the ground as if it weighs next to nothing.

Jax starts to cheer as we lift it off its pedestal. "Let's get out of—"

KABOOM!

The door to the atrium bursts off its frame, flying across the room and almost taking out half the kids. People dive out of the way as smoke bombs and spells fly everywhere, clouding the air with fire and smoke. In the haze, I see Stiltskin and his squad running, their wands raised. I reach for my bow and arrow, but slowly realize their wands aren't trained on us; they're aimed at the harp.

Before any of us can react, the Stiltskin Squad channels their power together. The harp begins to glow bright red as if it might burst into flames and sparks rain down on us as I pull AG and Anna behind my back. Stiltskin runs forward and points his wand at Alva's statue. It begins to glow red too, and a cold fear washes over me.

He's breaking her curse with the harp's help. *My* help!

"Someone stop that spell!" I shout.

Jax and Jocelyn run at Stiltskin, but his squad members are one step ahead of us. They're already shooting spells that send my friends flying backward. Maxine goes charging in next and is sent flying into a wall. Every time one of us comes at him, they zap us right back. I watch Kayla make her move. She flutters toward Rump with Ollie on her back. With Stiltskin's eyes on them, I run at him at full force and knock the wand out of the troll's hand. Someone bangs into the harp, and it crashes to the floor, breaking the connection to Alva. The room goes silent as the smoke and ash swirls around us.

We did it!

My eyes lock on Stiltskin, and a feeling of triumph comes over me. "Your plan failed."

"Did it?" Rumpelstiltskin's smile is pure evil as he reveals a mouth of gold teeth. He starts to laugh uncontrollably, showing off his hairy chin. The sound of his laughter is so high pitched and unnatural that it makes the hair on my arms stand up. Stiltskin Squad members join in on the laughter. "You foolish little girl. My plan didn't fail." His eyes narrow at me. "Yours did!"

I glance quickly at Alva's statue and realize it's no longer there.

I inhale sharply. In its place, a dark-haired woman is lying on the floor, her silky, black wings covering her like a cape. The Wicked Fairy is free.

I look at Rumpelstiltskin in horror and feel a spell hit me in the chest. The room around me swirls, then fades to black.

CHAPTER 17

The Battle between the Light and the Dark

The sound of my name brings me back to consciousness. "Gilly? Gilly, are you okay?" Someone is leaning over me—Anna? As the face comes into focus, I realize it's AG. I try to sit up, but I don't have the use of my hands. They're bound by invisible restraints, the same ones that now burn into AG's wrists. The fear on her face is easy to read. We're trapped.

I glance around the room to get a handle on the situation. The kids we just rescued are being wrangled together and tied with magical restraints. Squad members are placing the broken pieces of the harp in a large tin box while others attend to Alva, who is still lying motionless on the floor. One girl leans down and presses her ear to her chest.

"She's breathing!" says the girl.

"You may have reversed Alva's curse, but the harp is broken," I yell to Rump. "You'll never be able to enact your curse now."

"Oh, Gillian, you simple girl." Rumpelstiltskin looks like an old man as he dusts himself off and fixes the collar of his gold shirt. His beady eyes are as dark as ever. "Who said the harp needed to be in one piece in order to work its magic?" I freeze.

"All we needed was for someone pure of heart to make it play, and that someone was you!" Rumpelstiltskin explains, laughing harder. "My love for Alva may be strong, but it's tied up in our mutual desire to control Enchantasia. That's way too evil for the harp. That's where you came in!" He folds his hands across his wide belly. "We knew you wanted your poor, unfortunate sister back so you could save her from a life of villainy." His voice is mocking. "We just needed someone on the inside at FTRS to plant the seed that she was unhappy. And you came running!" He dances around the room. "What fun it's been watching you fall for every little trick we've planted!"

Someone on the inside? I don't understand. And then it dawns on me. I look at Jack. "You tricked me." He looks down. "I trusted you, defended you to my friends. I followed your lead." I feel like such a fool. "And the whole time, you've been working with him?"

"Yes," Jack says bluntly. "Look, I'm sorry, but I made a deal. Get you to come up here to play the harp in exchange for my mum and my cow back. I had no choice. It was just business."

"Business? You betrayed Enchantasia!" I shout, struggling against my binds.

"You seem nice enough," Jack tells me, and my mouth runs dry. "But it was your family or mine." He looks at Stiltskin. "Now it's time to uphold your end of the bargain."

"Bring out Mr. Spriggins's mum and cow," Stiltskin tells Gretel.

Gretel opens the door to the atrium. Jack's mum is in tears when she sees him. She runs to Jack, and they embrace.

"Now place them all together, like he wanted," Rump says. "The dungeon will suffice."

"The dungeon?" Jack spins around. "You said I'd get my mum and cow back!"

"And you have, haven't you? It's not my fault you never said *where* you wanted to end up with them. So the three of you will stay here and help me now."

Jack struggles as Gretel ties them all together. "You lied!

We had a deal." Gretel pushes the three of them over to our hostage area. "We had a deal!"

"You should have made a smarter one!" Stiltskin sneers, then looks at me again. "I have the harp thanks to you too. And now we can finally start putting our plan into action."

Rump thinks he's won, but he hasn't. "You won't get away with this. I've stopped you once. I'll do it again. I've already saved Anna. I can still save the harp too."

"Have you really saved Anna?" Rumpelstiltskin thinks for a moment. "Or did she never need saving?"

He's stumped me again. I turn and watch dumb-founded as Anna steps out of the hostage pool and walks over to Rumpelstiltskin. I feel like I've fallen fifty feet down the beanstalk.

"I'm sorry, Gilly." Her voice is suddenly cold. The tears that stained her face only moments are gone. "There was no way to break Alva's curse without your help, and we need Alva for what we have planned. Someday you'll see it's for the best." Someone hands Anna a fresh jacket and she slips out of the dirty one, which was clearly for my benefit. A girl hands her a comb, and Anna quickly smooths her locks and adds a headband. The *poor little Anna* routine is over.

"It was all a lie?" I ask. I feel like I might throw up. My sweet little sister is really gone. "You tricked me too?"

"We knew your love for me was pure enough to get the harp to play," Anna explains, her face brightening. "And it did. Now Rumpelstiltskin can cast the greatest curse Enchantasia has ever seen." She turns back toward me and touches my arm. I recoil. "Don't worry. Your life will be spared in the curse. I made sure he let me include you and our family when he remakes Enchantasia the way it was meant to be."

Hot tears fall down my cheeks. My baby sister has truly turned evil. I thought I could change her, but Professor Sebastian is right. People can only change if they want to. Thanks to my foolishness, I've endangered not only my friends, but also the whole kingdom. I should have listened to Jax. How could I be so pigheaded?

I steel myself as I look at Anna and say, "I don't want any part of your plan. I won't turn evil, Anna. Not even for you."

Anna rolls her eyes. "Oh, Gilly, always so concerned with being *good*. Well, guess what? Now I'm better than you ever were. I'm part of greatness! With Stiltskin and Alva's curse, Enchantasia will be great again. No troll and ogre war, no school for royals or schools for children who might become villains. Stiltskin will unite the whole kingdom. Under his rule, we will all matter! Villains won't dare attack us with him in charge. No one will be able to stop us."

Anna is clearly committed to this cause, but I have to try one more time. "The past is in the past," I say. "The only thing that can be changed is the future. Deep down, you must know how wrong this is."

Anna's face darkens. "What's wrong is you not seeing how much good he can do for all of us. Forget FTRS and these people!" She motions to my friends. "They're not your family. I am."

"We've acted more like her family these last few months than you ever have," Jocelyn snaps. "You're just too jealous to admit that to yourself."

"I have nothing to be jealous of!" Anna says, but her voice does sound shaky. "Gilly is the coward! She can't see the future!" Anna turns to Hansel. "Put them with the others and then get them all back down to the dungeons. They'll be out of our way down there."

The candy thief drags me back over to my friends. I'm too broken to fight him.

I watch Anna talking to Stiltskin as the squad members

continue to collect harp pieces. Alva is placed on a stretcher and removed from the room. Gretel rounds up the rest of us, zapping kids who don't move fast enough with her wand. I see a shadow cross her face and look up. Erp is still watching us, but no one seems to notice. If only I could get a message to him. But would he even help us?

A boy pats me down, searching for weapons. He pulls my coal miner dagger off me, then lifts my bow and arrow. I reach for it out of force of habit, but the kid throws it on to the pile of weapons he's already collected. The coal miner daggers we need to climb back down the beanstalk have all been taken. Ollie's and Jax's swords and Jocelyn's bag of magic tricks are gone too.

I look from Jack to Jax. "I'm sorry. You tried to tell me that I was being played by this kid, and I didn't listen. Now we're trapped here."

Jack cuts into our conversation and says, "Hey, I was played too. I had to put my family first. Didn't you do the same?"

"On some level," I admit. "But look at what it got me. I'm stuck in an atrium with a cow, a wicked fairy, and a sister who has turned evil." I look at Jax again. "I'm a fool."

Jax's face is sad. "I'm sorry I was right. I really wanted to be wrong."

I wish looking into his violet eyes would calm me like it has before. This time it doesn't. "I know."

Tears stream down AG's cheeks. "He's so evil," she whispers. "Father said he was, but I thought he could be reasoned with. Now I see for myself he can't. He'll never reverse my curse. He'll only try to strike another deal. What he did to you and your sister… I'm so sorry, Gilly."

"What curse?" Jocelyn asks. "This one is cursed too? How so?"

AG doesn't answer. She's crying too hard. I doubt she'd tell Jocelyn what she is anyway.

I look at the rest of my friends. "I'm sorry I dragged you all into my mess. I wish I knew how to get us out of it."

"Move!" Gretel barks, knocking me from behind. "Time for the dungeon! It's nice and damp down there. I'm sure you'll love the accommodations, pretty little princess."

She pokes AG with her wand and laughs, and AG growls.

"What did you just say to me?" Gretel gets in AG's face. "I said *move*! I'm not scared of any beast's daughter."

AG growls louder this time. Her chest is rising and falling heavily. She looks at me, a mixture of uncertainty and determination in her yellowing eyes. Maybe hope isn't lost yet.

"AG, be proud of who you are," I encourage her. "Own it!"

"Enough goody-goody talk." Gretel pushes me again. "Get walking. You and the pretty little princess."

"Don't call me a pretty little princess," AG says.

"Oh?" Gretel smiles slyly. "Why not?"

AG bares her teeth, which are starting to sharpen. "Because I am so much more."

I step back as AG's chest heaves harder and her body begins to twitch.

"Go, AG, go!" Maxine cries as the others look around in confusion.

"What's wrong with her?" Gretel asks as AG falls to her hands and knees and her back contorts. She writhes in pain as hair sprouts from her arms and legs and covers her whole body. Then she lets out a roar so fierce as she breaks through her restraints that it makes even my knees shake. AG lifts her head and locks her yellowed eyes on Gretel.

"She's a beast!" Gretel cries.

The pretty little princess is now full wolf. She pounces at Gretel, and Gretel screams. Squad members start running. Anna's jaw drops at the sight of the chaos.

"This is our chance," Jack tells us over the yelling. He opens his hand to reveal a magic bean. "It can get us out of here."

I don't ask where he got it or how long he's had it, but I still hesitate. Jack places the bean in my hands. "You're in charge, Gilly. I'm sorry about before. Tell the bean where you want to go, and we're there."

"No, I don't want that responsibility," I say and try to give the bean to Jax as AG continues to howl and charge through the room. "I don't deserve it."

"Just because you screwed up before doesn't mean you'll screw up now," Jax shouts. "Trust yourself!"

But I don't. Not around Anna. What if I think of the wrong place? What if we wind up stuck here?

"Gather everyone around," Jax tell the others. "Someone grab AG."

"AG!" Maxine whistles. "Here…um…girl!" AG comes running, and Maxine tackles her.

"What are they doing?" Hansel shouts, looking at the group of us, clinging to one another as other squad members, clearly terrified of AG, continue to hide.

Crash! Shards of glass begin to rain from the glass

ceiling. Erp has punched his hand through the ceiling. The remaining Stiltskin Squad members guarding the kids run for cover.

Now's our chance. I dive for the pile of weapons, grabbing my bow and arrow as Jax grabs Ollie's sword and swings it straight for Stiltskin. He rolls out of the way before it can hit him, but Anna is coming after me.

The sight of her trying to stop me is almost more than I can bear. Her face is so full of anger it looks…evil. I fire a warning shot in her direction and she drops to the floor, but then she bounces right back up and keeps coming. That girl is a fighter.

Jocelyn yanks me back as I fire off arrow after arrow, trying to keep Anna and Stiltskin down.

"They have the harp pieces!" Gretel points at Kayla and Jocelyn, who now have the tin box.

"Don't let them get away!" Anna cries. "Block the exits! They have nowhere to escape!"

"That's what you think, traitor!" Jocelyn shouts.

Jax and Ollie gather Jack, his mum and cow, and the other kids around the tin box. Maxine holds tight to a thrashing AG. I hold the bean tightly in my now sweaty hand.

"Erp!" I hear Kayla shout as his hand reaches through the ceiling for our group. "Get us out of here!" Squad members begin wanding spells at him, but Erp's hand keeps coming. Kids gather tight around the box, some climbing on top to make our group as compact as possible.

Rumpelstiltskin reaches for his wand. He aims at us, and this time I know he's not hoping to stun. But before he can fire off a spell, Erp scoops us up and lifts us through the ceiling. I feel a pang of regret as I look down to see Anna's face turn ghostly white. "No!" she screams. But as we clear the building, I know I have to leave Anna behind. Not because I want to, but because she has to figure this out on her own.

Erp sets us down on a cloud and crouches next to us. I can hear the commotion behind us. They'll be out of the building and here any second.

"*Now!*" Jocelyn shouts, and I get ready to throw down the bean.

Take us home, I think.

The bean explodes, shattering into a thousand pieces, each one radiating a bright-white light. The break is followed by a loud gush of wind that threatens to pull us all apart. We hold on tight as a swirling vortex of clouds spins around us, tight like a funnel. Below them, I see the leaves of a beanstalk start to form. There is another bright flash of light, a screeching sound, and we're gone.

CHAPTER 18

Unhappily After...for Now

W hen I open my eyes, all I see are blue sky and clouds. Am I still in Cloud City?

I sit up fast and feel dizzy.

"Oh, my head," I hear Jax moan. Children all around me are coming to as well. I look around.

We are scattered on the ground like bread crumbs, each one of us lying near a twisting, turning root of a fresh, new beanstalk. Everyone looks as dazed and confused as I am, especially when they see Erp lying in a giant-sized crater on the ground.

I am not home in my cozy boot, but I am back at Fairy Tale Reform School, safely on the ground. I smile. My head won out over my heart.

A sound like thunder rumbles through the ground as the staff bursts from the school, trailed by dozens of students aiming weapons. They look from the new beanstalk to Erp, who is trying to stand, to the kids scattered across the ground.

Tessa lowers her wand in surprise. "It's Gilly and the others!" she cries, and everyone lets up a loud cheer. "They're okay!"

Rapunzel lowers her crossbow and runs to Jax. "It *is* you!" He's still just sitting up when Rapunzel tackles him in a hug.

It's like a domino effect. Jack, his mum, and Milky Way have a reunion on a vine. Kayla flies to her mother's and sisters' sides, then drags them over to meet Erp as she starts telling everyone how he helped save us. Ollie and Blackbeard trade sword-fighting stories. Maxine and AG hug their fellow RLWs.

Students run over to the rescued kids, offering their mini magic mirrors so the kids can reach home and tell their parents they've been found. Even non-FTRS kids seem happy to have someone kind and forgiving wrap a blanket or cloak around them.

"No candy!" I hear a goblin boy beg. "All I've eaten for the past month is candy. It's fun for the first week, but if

I ever see a lavender gumdrop again, I think I'll have the shakes."

It should be a happy moment, but I can't help thinking about the one person who didn't come back with us.

"Jocelyn!" snaps Professor Harlow. She's busy putting up some sort of shield that keeps sputtering out and dying every time she casts it. "Stop lollygagging and help me with this blocking charm! It takes two, and we don't want to let anyone through!"

Jocelyn, who appears to have face-planted, attempts to stand and staggers over to Harlow to help her. Seconds later, the two of them manage to cross magic streams and send a glowing bubble up over the beanstalk, preventing anyone or anything from climbing it till it can be cut down.

"What about the giant?" someone cries as Erp finally stands and starts to stumble around. "Someone restrain him!"

"No!" Jack shouts, rushing forward. He steps onto Erp's mega-sized toes. "Erp is harmless. I can't speak for all giants, but Erp helped save us." He hangs his head as he looks at his mum and Milky Way. "It was my fault everyone needed saving though. I got myself thrown into FTRS on purpose so I could get close to Gilly and convince her to go after Anna."

"Sweetheart, why would you do that?" his mother asks.

Jack pauses again. "Because I was working with Rumpelstiltskin."

The outcry is loud and angry and all at once.

"Young man, explain yourself at once," Headmistress Flora demands. She sounds angry, but I know she'll be fair with Jack. He may have tricked us, but he did help us escape. And if he's willing to change, then maybe he deserves a place at FTRS.

But right now, I need to be alone to think about all that's happened since I climbed into the sky to save my sister and came back empty-handed. I walk away from the crowd and sit under a large oak tree with my back to the school. I close my eyes for a moment, listening to the sound of the wind.

"Gilly?" I hear a gruff yet tentative voice say. "Mind if I join you?"

It's Allison Grace, who is still partially in wolf form.

"How'd you know where I was?" I ask, looking back at where Jack is speaking to the crowd.

AG points to her snout. I mean nose. I mean snout-nose. "Powerful sniffer. You've got a strong scent."

"Oh. Thanks. I think."

AG sits down next to me, and neither of us says anything for a while. Then I hear someone calling her name.

"Allison Grace!" Beauty cries when she sees AG sitting with me. "Kayla said you came back, but when we didn't see you, we feared the worst. Oh, and, sweetheart, you're…" No one will say the word *beast* in front of her.

Prince Sebastian and Beauty quickly try to cover her with a cloak.

"No, I'm not hiding who I am anymore!" AG pushes off the blanket, surprising them both. She stands up unsteadily, and I get a good look at the princess in all her wolfy glory. "Yes," she growls, her voice gravelly, "I'm cursed to be part princess and part beast, but I'm not afraid of my beast side anymore. I think being part beast makes me a princess you won't want to tangle with. And I like that."

Beauty and the prince look at each other doubtfully. Then he trains his eyes on me.

"Did you convince our daughter to go on this foolish quest and risk her life?" he thunders.

"Don't blame Gilly, Father," AG interrupts. "I made the choice. Gilly is my friend—a good friend—and I wanted to help her try to get her sister back. If I hadn't transformed, we might not have escaped Stiltskin." The prince starts to growl.

"Er—maybe I should let you three to catch up," I say, anxious to avoid the prince's wrath.

The prince puts out a hand to stop me. "You stay right here."

"Sebastian, the girl just lost her sister!" Beauty says. "Hasn't she been through enough?"

"Don't get mad," AG tells the prince. "Your job is to be my father, not the Dwarf Police Squad. I don't want to be cut off from the world anymore. Why should I be ashamed of who I am just because you were ashamed of your appearance? My beast side can come in handy."

"Or it will get you shunned," the prince says.

"People are more accepting now," AG says as her body starts to transform back. The hair is starting to recede from her body as she slowly becomes human again. "If I show them there is nothing to fear about me being different, then they won't be afraid. Being different is what makes us special. That's what Gilly taught me. I need to own my differences, not hide them."

Prince Sebastian looks at me ever so briefly. "Gillian Cobbler taught you that?

"It seems like this is a much longer discussion that we should have," the prince tells his daughter, "and we will have it when we get home. To the pop-up castle."

"You mean we're not going *home* home?" AG asks excitedly.

The prince looks from Beauty to his daughter. "It would appear we are home. I've never seen you more comfortable than you are here." AG jumps up and hugs him. "All your mother and I want is for you to be safe and happy. And if that means staying here, then here we'll stay."

"Fiddlesticks," I say under my breath. "I guess this means I still have to finish my family tree."

The prince surveys me with pursed lips. "Perhaps we could work on that together," he says, to my surprise. "It appears you and I have more in common than I realized. We should get together to talk about Rumpelstiltskin someday soon."

"Really?" I ask in surprise.

"Really." The prince almost smiles.

Jocelyn whistles for us. Everyone under the beanstalk is staring. "Hey! You two. Want to come join the party? We have a crazed villain on the loose to deal with, you know."

AG, Beauty, Prince Sebastian, and I walk back over to where the others are gathered.

Headmistress Flora's face is grave. "We must alert the royal court and the Dwarf Police Squad immediately. They will want to prepare for any situation."

Tessa and Raza both are in hysterics. "Our beloved Princess Rose! She's just getting her strength back at her summer retreat. If she hears of Alva's return, it will send her straight back to bed!"

"Or back to plotting her takeover of the royal court," Jocelyn mumbles. This *almost* makes me laugh.

"For now, we will let Rapunzel and the royal court worry about Princess Rose's needs," Flora says delicately. "We have children to return to their worried parents, and all of you need a good long rest. Off to bed!"

Our group starts to disperse, but I find I'm not sleepy. I'm not ready to end the day just yet, and Flora knows it.

I put up my hand. "You don't have to say it," I tell her. "I know what I did was headstrong and selfish."

"And foolish!" Jocelyn adds.

"And brave," AG adds. Everyone looks at her.

"I'm with Jocelyn," I tell her. "I was foolish. All I cared about was finding Anna and convincing her to come home. I wanted her to change so badly." I look at all my professors.

"But my sister is a full-blown villain now. I've accepted it, and I won't make the same mistake twice."

"Maybe she is, and maybe she isn't," Jack says softly, and we all look at him standing with Erp. "I worked for Stiltskin too, didn't I? And I lured you up the beanstalk to help him just like Anna did, but now I'm standing here with you instead of him. People can change if they really want to."

"Jack's right," AG agrees. "Look how much I've changed since I've met you! I never thought I'd be okay with being part beast. But now I own it." She winks at me, and I grin.

"A villain is only a villain because they know no other way to be," Jax says. "There's still hope for Anna."

"And if she doesn't change?" Maxine whispers.

I look up at the blue sky again and take a deep breath. "If she can't, then we'll still do whatever it takes to stop her and Rumpelstiltskin." I look at Jax, who begins to smile. "We have a kingdom to save."

Acknowledgments

Kate Prosswimmer, thank you for being my partner in all things Fairy Tale Reform School–related. You are my lifeline and sounding board, and I couldn't go on these journeys without you! To Team Sourcebooks—Beth Oleniczak, Heather Moore, Alex Yeadon, Kathryn Lynch, Todd Stocke, Sean Murray—thank you for all you do for this world. You've made it bigger and better than I ever could have imagined. I don't know how you do it, Mike Heath, but I love each cover design you create more than the last! Thanks for making FTRS come alive! Special thanks to Diane Danneneldt, Gretchen Stelter, and Elizabeth Boyer for keeping me on point.

For Dan Mandel, you always have my back, and I'm forever grateful. And for Kieran Scott, Elizabeth Eulberg, and

Courtney Sheinmel, thank you for being there for my every fairy tale need and for keeping me sane.

Mike, Tyler, and Dylan, I couldn't do what I do without your love and support. It's because of you three, I get to go on this wild adventure that I love so much. And to my parents, Lynn and Nick Calonita for your unwavering love and cheerleading.

And to the bookstores, libraries, and readers who have embraced Fairy Tale Reform School, I'm so grateful you've found this series and enjoy reading it as much as I enjoy writing it! I am so thankful to have you all in my corner!